Richa

Ned Locksley, the Etonian

Vol. II

SALZWASSER
VERLAG

Richard Seymour C. Chermside

Ned Locksley, the Etonian

Vol. II

Reprint of the original, first published in 1863.

1st Edition 2022 | ISBN: 978-3-37500-134-6

Verlag (Publisher): Salzwasser Verlag GmbH, Zeilweg 44, 60439 Frankfurt, Deutschland
Vertretungsberechtigt (Authorized to represent): E. Roepke, Zeilweg 44, 60439 Frankfurt, Deutschland
Druck (Print): Books on Demand GmbH, In de Tarpen 42, 22848 Norderstedt, Deutschland

NED LOCKSLEY,

THE ETONIAN;

OR,

THE ONLY SON.

IN TWO VOLUMES.

VOL. II.

LONDON

1863.

NED LOCKSLEY, THE ETONIAN.

CHAPTER I.

Queens of society in Freshet, the Miss Davenants ruled, after all, a narrow court circle. Keane's energy and ability distinguished him within it only too easily and too favourably. Being neither ill-favoured nor ill-mannered—for his selfishness was of that dangerous kind which can keep itself, at need, under vigilant self-control—he was well received by the Davenants, when, for the sake of such social distinction as it might give him, he sought their closer acquaintance. At first he divided his attentions between them with strict impartiality. Sophy's careless good nature allowed him to gain with her a certain familiar footing, beyond which he did not care to adventure. He inclined to think her prettier than her sister; but Fanny's greater reserve roused, by degrees, his innate love of predominance. Without setting much value on the prize itself, should it be won, he could not resist the pleasure of striving for the mastery. Like a cautious engineer, he opened his first parallel at safe distance—so safe, that Fanny was in doubt whether his advances were insidious, or simply deferential. She felt but little attraction or liking towards Keane; but there was this affinity between them, that her temper had in it also some love of a mere struggle, finding therein a satisfaction apart from the resulting issue. It nettled her to feel, as she was dimly conscious of feeling, a little afraid of Keane. This consciousness provoked her to acquiesce in the growth of an intimacy against which, now and then, she would almost determine. She was not the girl to desire direct compliments to her person or her mind; yet Keane had wit enough to offer a continual and subtle flattery. Her education, though imperfect, had been ambitious, and had roused intellectual aspirations which there was little to satisfy in the common tone of the young men around her.

Keane noted and profited by this. His acuteness readily caught up hints of the drift of her thought and study; and his lawyer-like ability in getting up a subject enabled him to win from her considerable respect for his own attainments, whilst paying in conversation a delicate deference to hers.

Thus matters stood between them up to the time of their chance meeting that afternoon on the Lanercost road. Neither the sisters nor Keane suspected what influence his drive to that village was to exercise upon their future. Keane of course knew, what the sisters did not, and what with professional caution he kept from them, that he was driving thither in answer to a summons from their own aunt, Miss Davenant. She was a queer, little old lady, whose cheeks had kept a sort of streaky withered bloom, such as some apples keep long after Christmas time. Her eyes were bright and restless; her little figure erect; her footstep light and quick; her voice thin and clear. She was counted neither very sociable nor very shy; neither very amiable nor very cross; neither very rich nor very poor. She lived in a cottage ráther smaller than her estimated income might have warranted, but for her combined love of cats and china. The crashes which her animate pets produced at times among her pets of still-life never disturbed her temper, so equally were her affections balanced between them; but they must frequently have produced a crisis in her exchequer. The broken porcelain was always replaced, no matter at what cost of money or of trouble, as exactly as circumstances would allow. One rule was invariable: if no perfectly resembling substitute was to be found, at least no inferior was ever tolerated. Exchange, like that of glebe land, must be for the better or not at all; the novelty must needs be costlier than the loss it repaired.

"Keane, my dear," said the little old lady after the first civilities had passed between them, "you must tell your groom to put up at the Swan. Your horse can't wait about all the afternoon. I shall keep you some time."

He went towards the door to give his man directions.

"But Keane, my dear, the man shan't sit in the tap-room. Tell him he may come in here to tea, if he don't smell of tobacco."

Keane was not so very much surprised at her terms of endearment. Though he had never had much to do with her, he had known her all his life; and she had on all occasions taken a caressing tone towards him. But when his dog-cart had driven off, and he was seated on a very slight stiff seat in the drawing-room—for Miss Davenant sat in one arm-chair, and three puffy kittens, on no account to be disturbed, were nestled on the other—she suddenly accosted him in terms which almost made him open his eyes wide, an unusual practice with him.

"Keane, my dear, you may not be aware that you ought by rights to have been my son, and not your mother's."

"Indeed!" he said, not without misgivings as to the old lady's sanity.

"You may well say 'indeed;' but Isabella Keane—Burkitt that now is—knows it as well as I do."

"You don't mean to say so, my dear madam?" said Keane; because he couldn't think of any thing on earth to say.

"I always say what I mean," she answered primly.

This was not to be gainsaid, so Keane held his peace.

"Not that your dear father and I were ever positively engaged," she resumed, "nor indeed that he ever made me exactly an offer; but I always have thought, and will think, that it was in his mind to do so, till he came across Isabella Keane, your mother that now is."

The old lady spoke in the most matter-of-fact way, as if Keane had really undergone a change of maternal parentage.

"What's more, it was always in my mind, and is so, to have accepted him when he should ask me; so that I *should* have been your mother, Keane, my dear, by right, you see."

Sane or not, she was perfectly self-possessed. No emotion seemed to quiver in her chirping little voice.

"I always loved your father as long as he was alive; and I have always liked you for his sake, since you were born; not your mother though. But I forgave her, a little bit, when she lost poor James."

The kittens woke up, and began a game of romps, during which one of them rolled on to the floor.

"Poor, dear little pussy!" cried Miss Davenant, catching it up and fondling it.

"The long and short of it is, my dear, that I want to make my will; and as I hear you are a first-rate man of business now, and as I think you will deal fairly with me for your father's sake, I have sent for you to tell me how to set about it."

This was coming to the point, and was a great relief to Keane, who produced a pocket-book.

"I am sure, dear madam, I deeply feel your personal kindness towards me, and you will find, I trust, that, professionally, your confidence is not misplaced. If you will allow me to take down the heads of your intentions, that is, unless you may have memoranda of your own prepared, eh? No. Then, as I said, I will take down rough notes, put them into shape to-morrow or next day, and do myself the honour of waiting upon you with a draft."

"Yes, well, I suppose you *will* have to do something of the sort, my dear. But not quite so straight off: though I have no doubt you are very clever at business matters: your father always was. There's a good deal to get at—about these Mexican mines, for instance."

"Yes, a bad business most times. I hope you have not been 'bitten hard,' as we say in business."

"Oh, dear me, no; my mines turned out well for a wonder. Most of those which didn't, I sold when they were well thought of. Then I have other whatyoumaycall'em, 'security,' things of different sorts. I believe you'll find I'm very rich, my dear, when all's reckoned."

"I am sure I hope I may; but nine times out of ten, when I look into people's money matters I find them poorer than they took themselves to be."

"That's not the case with me, you may depend upon it. Shall you have time to look through my papers, or will you do it another day?"

"No time like the present," said the cautious Keane, looking at his watch. "We don't dine till eight; and if we did, they know my ways too well to wait for me, when I am over office hours."

"Come into the dining-room, then. You shall have short-bread and sherry whilst you look through the documents in my tin case."

It was of the shape and size of many on Burkitt and Goring's shelves; but heavier than he had expected. As he lifted it from under the sideboard on to the dining-room table, it crossed his mind that there might be china plates packed up in it. Miss Davenant's name was in fat white letters outside.

Fidgeting in her pocket for the key of the padlock, she said—

"My poor old man of business, that was, is dead, up in London, and I wouldn't let strangers have anything to do with my affairs; so I sent for the box, and here it is. I can trust you, my dear, I feel, for your father's sake."

But when the lid was open, Keane opened his eyes again, wider and wider after inspection of every fresh handful of papers and parchments.

"Why, Miss Davenant, excuse me, your man of business was a very good one; or you are a very good woman of business yourself."

"A little of both, perhaps. I have never been extravagant in any thing but porcelain."

There was no confusion. All was docketed, endorsed, and ticketed: all tied with pink tapes, some pale with age, some with the blush of recent manufacture on them. Long before Keane had feund his way to the under layers with the most faded ties, he was fairly overwhelmed with astonishment at the old woman's wealth."

"Excuse me, my dear madam; but I had no idea your property was so considerable."

"No, nor had anybody, but me and my old man of business, that's dead and gone, you know. No one shall have now, but you and me, my dear."

"You may count, of course, on my discretion as on your own, Miss Davenant."

"Just so, my dear. Do you like the carraway

comfits on the short bread, or the bits of candied lemon best, eh?"

"Varanas Viejas! Why, my dear madam, those are the best things in 'silvers' going now-a-days. I saw them, only yesterday, quoted at a stunning premium in the *Times'* City article. One, two, three, four, five, of the *original* 'coupons' too. How on earth did you get hold of them?"

"Ah, well never mind that now, my dear. They were in a bad way once, after Garboga's insurrection, I can tell you. But you are too young even to have heard of that. Good little Mr. Gossett lost heart himself about them, and said I might make them into spills to light my taper with; but I didn't you see: and I was right, and he was wrong, my dear."

Keane gave her a look of unfeigned respect and admiration, not so much even for the wealth, as for the wit that had won it.

She brought him pen, ink, and paper, for the matter had grown beyond the limits of his little pocket-book, and he proceeded with an enumeration of the different valuable securities.

"I never use all my dividends," she said, when it was drawing to a close; "so the banker's book shows a balance, as you shall see."

A balance, indeed! Whose could such expectations be? "I must next ask, whether your intended dispositions are intricate, Miss Davenant?"

"Oh, dear, no. The simplest in the world. There are the cats; of course I shall do nothing extravagant or eccentric for them. I've never been reckoned either, and don't mean to be when I'm dead and gone, you know. Seventy pounds a-year each to my own maid, my cook, and housemaid. They three must divide any surviving cats between them, and shall have £5 a-year for each pussy for its lifetime. That's moderate. Then there's yourself."

Keane looked up and fairly stared this time. His very pulses quickened.

"Yes, I shall leave you just £1,000 for every year that I may live after the will is signed, my dear. The more years I live the larger figures before the noughts, you know. I shouldn't like you to long for my death at all. See you make that part clear, eh."

"And the bulk of the property, Miss Davenant?"

"No, not so fast, my dear, there's the china. Who shall have the china? I should be almost as sorry to have it badly treated as the cats. Do you know any one who is fond of old china? Not your mother. I know she is; but I haven't quite forgiven her to that extent. There's your aunt, now, your father James's sister, Lucy, does she like old china, think you?"

"To be sure she does, intensely," said Keane, who knew nothing at all about it; but thought he might get credit with Aunt Lucy sooner or later for the legacy.

"Well, your Aunt shall have it. Lucy Burkitt that was, Locksley that now is; put that down."

"All right, madam. And the bulk of the property?"

"Will be divided of course, between my two nieces, Fanny and Sophy Davenant."

Well might he determine on doubly gilt gold letters for "The Sisters" on the stern of his redecorated sailing-boat.

"Equally divided, I presume, dear madam?"

"Wrong, my dear, as nine presumptions out of ten are. I shall make an heiress; for I detest equality. It's a French revolutionary notion. And I look upon all such as wicked and—bloodthirsty."

"Gold-thirsty would seem to fit this case better than blood-thirsty, Miss Davenant," said Keane, affecting jocularity to hide the tremulous concern which had come upon him, succeeding the wild expectation that the mention of his own name had roused. Of which sister would she make an heiress? That was indeed a momentous question. Though she could not suspect that he had any, the remotest, personal interest in asking; yet he feared to betray himself to her in putting the next necessary question.

"It shall be two-thirds to one of the girls: only one to the other," she said.

"It will, of course, be necessary to specify which of the young ladies is to take the larger share under the will, Miss Davenant."

"Certainly. But there's no need to put any names in the draft. They can be filled in after. I don't know that I've made my mind up yet."

"I should have thought you were a stickler for 'primogeniture,' Miss Davenant, with your anti-French revolutionary feelings."

"There's something in that, my dear: a good deal, indeed. 'First come first served:' sound enough sense, I say."

"And your executors?"

"Yourself and the girl's father, my youngest

brother, George: indeed my only remaining one. A bit more short bread, or another glass of sherry?"

"No, thank you, though both are excellent. What day would be convenient for me to wait upon you with the rough copy of the draft?"

"Any: the sooner the better. Remember there's one thing I must insist upon."

"Which is?"

"The strictest secrecy. I don't want my nieces to be wishing me dead any more than yourself, my dear."

"Do I look like a man to let a client's affairs leak out, Miss Davenant?"

The little old lady eyed him curiously, then said at last:

"Not a bit, my dear."

Keane's dog-cart was soon bowling home again. French revolutionists did indeed abolish the laws of primogeniture. Miss Davenant thought those revolutionists both wicked and blood-thirsty. Mr. Keane Burkitt stood upon some vantage ground, though never so narrow, with Miss Fanny Davenant. That young lady was her aunt's elder niece. A man of business has many things to think about. They seemed to reach the town turn-pike in no time. Yet when he got home his uncle and aunt both said:

"You have nearly starved us all, Keane, you are so late home to dinner, to-day."

CHAPTER II.

Not quite sunk in the languor of older lady residents, Rosa Barrington and her cousin Florence were yet somewhat exhausted by the fatigues of last night's entertainment at Government House.

The cool season, though not quite over—" Rosa dear, what will the warm be?"—was yielding daily to the growing ardours of an Indian sun. Wet mats of reed were dripping in the verandah; in the room punkahs never ceased to swing. The mails would be made up to-morrow. A ream of "India-post" on either open desk told of good resolutions concerning letters "home." But the pens lay idle, and the fair surface of the paper showed no stain of ink.

"Rosa, for shame!" cried Florence, "Indianising at this hour, after all your good intentions, too."

"Only this once, Flo; we don't dance every night."

His Excellency's daughter drew up therewith her feet on a divan, cushioned as for any Rajah's zenana.

"Happily not," answered her cousin, "and shall soon give over dancing altogether."

"Don't say 'happily,' dancing is my delight. It is a sad season that stops it. But I like your admonishing me for idleness—out of your easy chair!"

"Easy chair, indeed! A Chinese caricature of one. Knotty bamboo, to crumple one's barège, and make dints in one's back. Very different from your divan!"

"Change with me, then."

"Thanks, it's too much trouble."

"You Sybarite! The bamboo knots are crumpled rose-leaves. You know your cane is cooler than my cushions."

Florence laughed.

"Hadn't we some new faces here last night?" said Rosa.

"New shawls, dear. Was ever any thing like that little Cashmere chief's?"

"They said he was a Ghoorka from Nepaul."

"Perhaps he was; but his shawls were from Cashmere."

"One sees too many shawls, Flo, to care for them out here. What funny little pig's eyes the chief himself had, like a Chinaman's! When I spoke of faces I meant European, of course."

"Why 'of course,' pray? Don't you count Indian features, faces?"

"What! N, i, g—nig—"

"No, Rosa!" she cried, springing up in her eagerness from her bamboo seat of ease, "you shall not stain your rosy lips with such vile words!" She crossed the room towards her cousin with a gesture of reproof, earnest under playfulness. "Leave such heartless quips to rattlepate ensigns and raw civilians. I know the style of lad from whom you catch them up. They will know better before they command a regiment or sit in a magistrate's chair. As for you, you are the daughter of a British governor, ruling millions of these dusky-faced men, and should know better than to scorn those over whom your father rules!"

"What heroics! And you look as black as

thunder, or as Kali, the goddess fiend of your friends the nig—. Oh, dear me, no! Have mercy and pity on me, Flo dear, and I will say the dusky millions of Hindostan—indeed I will!" She clasped her hands together, enforcing their appeal with her prettiest look of deprecation. Very pretty, too, as she was herself. Florence gave the lightest admonitory tap to the fair forehead, saying, as she "kissed the place to make it well"—

"Giddy brain, but good heart, I believe!"

"But the new faces, Flo—the pale not the dusky—let us talk them over a bit before we set to work on our letters."

"Do you mean what Willie Sangster calls 'the griffs,' dear? Pale is hardly the right epithet for their cheeks yet. Your noisy partner in the last quadrille, for instance."

"What, Mr. O'Brien, with the brogue? I thought him charming—so good-humoured."

"Yes, but as pale as a peony!"

"Cherry-cheeked I must own; but quick as a flash of lightning. Such Irish sparkle in his eyes! Who were you dancing with, by-the-by? You were our *vis-à-vis*."

"A Mr. Lockyer, I think, or Lockery—I didn't quite hear when he was introduced."

"Who introduced him?"

"Oh, young Milward."

"And who may young Milward be, that we have his name off-hand already?"

"A boy I had met a few times at home. His mother is a widow and knows the Dalrymples. His sisters are very nice girls they say."

"Is *he* a very nice boy?"

"A very nice-looking one; but with features fitted for a girl, so fine and delicate."

"How glad he must have been to come across a home-county-ball partner in Bombay."

"Perhaps. But I think he voted me slow, so handed me over to his friend to be rid of me. He said, 'I think you'll find him in your line, Miss Barrington.'"

"And did you?"

"He's graver and more thoughtful than the general run of 'griffs,' no doubt. He owned that he was not much of a dancer. And it's my private belief he'll owe his friend a grudge for setting him to dance attendance on your humble servant."

"Nonsense, Flo. The poor griff was overcome by his unexpected promotion. What! a chance introduction gain him our queenly Florence's hand on his first night at Government House! Depend upon it he was nervous."

"I saw no symptoms. And yet"—

"Yet what, your Majesty? Now, no evasions," said Rosa, sitting up on the divan and holding up her finger. "It's my turn to be wiseacre, and I caution you against all concealment from your best friend and adviser."

Florence laughed again; but a bright blush on her countenance deepened as she seemed to collect her thoughts.

"Own at once, my dear Miss Florence, what that was which struck you in the air and address of this solemn young griff as indicative of—I really don't know what. No subterfuge, and no mock modesty!"

"I don't know—perhaps it was a fancy. When young Milward, in passing, took him by the arm and introduced him, asking me—the cool young monkey—to give his friend the next quadrille, he took no notice of me with his eyes, but held his arm out as the first bars were playing. When, once in position, he roused himself as 'an officer and a gentleman' to make small talk, I fancied I saw something start back in him when his eyes met mine. In him, remember—he never flinched one hair's-breadth."

"Well, after that?"

"After that he seemed annoyed at me—not a bit afraid—but as if anxious to give me no more fixed looks."

Rosa shook her head with amazing gravity.

"Very serious this for the solemn griff—unless, indeed, as your friend young Milward says, you should find him in your line, Miss Barrington."

"If you talk nonsense, Rosa, you shall hear no more of the whims which cross my fancy."

"Whims and fancies, indeed! As if Queen Florence ever had either!"

Apparently overpowered by so preposterous an idea, she threw herself back upon the cushions and closed her eyes. Florence also lay back in her cane chair as luxuriously as it would let her. A little creaking from the punkahs now and then enlivened the drip, drip, drip, from the mattings outside, but other sound there was none, and the cousins were half asleep.

A jaunty step, with a ring of spurs in the stone corridor outside, aroused them presently.

"Holloa there, you young ladies!"

The intrusion was, seemingly, not unexpected. Neither stirred hand nor foot, nor opened, perceptibly, an eyelid on the intruder.

"Poor darlings!" cried his voice, with affected sentiment. "They sleep! Sleep, all unwitting of the blight which descends on their young lives!"

He advanced, bent over each in turn, shaking his head mournfully at either. Then sunk upon a seat, and, as if overcome by sorrow, hid his face in a long muslin streamer which hung from a queer sort of turban on his head, pretending to sob aloud. This was more than Rosa could stand. She sat upright on her divan suddenly, and made a switch at him with a fly-flapper of palm leaf.

"The best and dearest girls! And both so fond, so very, very, fond of me, too! Both bereaved at twelve hours' notice. Oh, sad, sad!"

"Now don't be a goose, Willie," cried Rosa. "What are you at?"

"Poor little darling, hear its prattle, its pretty prattle, unconscious of bereavement, utterly!"

"If you go on so, Willie, I'll muster strength to throw this cushion at you, that I will, spite of Princess Propriety shamming sleep there in her bamboo chair."

"Now, Rosa," cried the princess, shocked at this outrageous menace, "you shall not throw cushions, even at Willie, like a romping tomboy, or I'll tell her Excellency."

"Sorrow for her, too," groaned the turbaned intruder. "Heart agonies in store, spite of her little hoard of maxims preaching down a cousin's heart."

"Really, Willie, you are intolerable," said Florence.

"Am I?" asked the offender, in the cheeriest tone imaginable, dropping his muslin weeper and readjusting his disordered mustachioes. "Wait till you hear my news, Miss Florence, and tell me whether that is tolerable. Good morning, Rosey; you're pretty when you pout."

"And you're ugly any way," said Rosa, which, on the whole, was true, though the aide-de-camp's ugliness was of the bright, manly, kindly sort.

"How she admires me!" he said, turning to Florence, "and conceals her infatuation under a thin disguise of irony. Oh, dear, oh, dear!"

"Now do be sensible, Willie," said Florence, "and if you have any thing to tell us tell it, without any more of this."

"What will not female flippancy dare?" he retorted. "Advise me to be sensible, me, whom the Brahmins consider an Avatar of good sense, whom the very Mussulmans have offered to make a Moollah if I would only dye my turban green! Sensible, indeed, what next?"

"You may well say what next when *you* turn sensible," said Rosa, springing off the sofa to threaten him at close quarters with the fly-flapper.

"Now, Rosa, sit down again this moment," said Florence, drawing her gently down on the divan beside herself. "Then we shall hear whether he *has* any thing to say."

"You are a learned lady, Florence," he resumed gravely, producing a couple of little medicine bottles from his coat pocket, and handing one to each of his cousins; for he, too, was a nephew of His Excellency the Governor. "You have a tinge of Latin, and can explain to poor, dear, ignorant little Rosey the use of lachrymatories among the ancients. Tear-bottles, dear child,—tear-bottles—the only two the Sub-inspector of Hospitals could spare this morning, though I told him you would want them larger."

"Oh, don't be tiresome and absurd, dear Willie," Rosa said, submissively, clasping her hands as she had done when deprecating Florence's playful anger.

"Tiresome! When I am trying to spare your feelings and break it to you by degrees!"

"Break what?"

"The dreadful tidings, to be sure."

"Tidings of what?"

"Of my departure for Calcutta by dâk to-morrow morning."

"Is that all?"

"All, indeed! Now, don't faint or scream, dears!"

"Upon my word now, Willie, it's too bad of you"—

"I know it is. You'll break your hearts, I fear, the pair of you. And then His Excellency, my poor dear uncle, just as I was teaching him his trade of governorship, poor man; he will be lost without me. There's one comfort though, his plans for irrigation might be started now. The tears of the young ladies of Bombay would fill a tank alone, to say nothing of the general weeping population, native and European."

"How long shall you be gone, Willie?"

"Ah, my poor dears, bear up, I'm going for good and all."

There was a touch of real feeling in the still bantering tone of the last sentence, and both the girls looked grave.

"You don't really mean that, Willie?" asked Florence, now with true concern.

"I do indeed, though. It is felt that the

Governor-General himself needs leading strings, even more than your dear papa, Miss Rosey. There is but one hand fit to hold them here in India," and he gracefully waved his own. "Wherefore I depart by dâk to-morrow morning before sunrise, obedient to superior orders, though they may lacerate your tender hearts."

"Now, tell us the real truth about it, Willie."

"Well, the real truth is, that I belong to the Bengal Presidency by rights, as you know. I was only acting aide-de-camp here to my uncle till my leave was up. But you also know I have been a bit in the Public Works line as well as the 'right shoulders, march,' business; and there's a canal opening immediately, for which I may be of use, and am recalled at once, accordingly."

This was a modest way of stating the fact. Willie Sangster, a thorough soldier, as a gash across his left cheek witnessed, had a remarkable genius for engineering, though not belonging to a scientific corps. He was wanted not only for the formal completion of a work in which he had borne a main part, but for its immediate and large extension. The despatch which summoned him from his pleasant duties on his uncle's staff was written in terms of which many an older officer and public servant might have been proud. He was more sorry, perhaps, to leave the company of his cousins than he cared to show, so he fell to "chaffing" them again.

"I wish to leave a parting gift with each of you. The same in either case. For worlds I would not bring fierce jealousies between you. Promise me that it shall not be so."

"We promise," cried Rosa; "what is it, Willie?"

"I wish to leave with each of you," he said, "a lock of my dear hair. Here, Rosey, sever two, but with impartial scissors. Neither must have a longer nor fuller curl than the other."

Therewith he pulled off his queer turban, exhibiting a pate shaven as smooth as the soft cheek of either cousin.

"If you had but one lock left wouldn't I have pulled it, for your impertinence!" cried she.

Florence's finger went up at her again.

"I would, Miss Flo, for all your finger-shaking. He's made a worse fright of himself than ever now."

"There's no pleasing you both. Florence entreats me to be sensible; obedient to the obvious teaching of good sense, I shave my head for a hot journey, as any native Indian might, whereon Miss

Rosey says I've made myself a fright. Well, never mind, all will be over soon between us."

"I have more than half a mind to cry, Willie," said Rosa, quite in earnest.

"And Florence more than two-thirds of a mind, I hope," he answered, looking more keenly at her than before. She gave no sign, however. "The worst of all is, I shall be supplanted in your esteem and admiration, perhaps, by the new aide-de-camp, though I am convinced your affection must remain unalterable."

"The new aide-de-camp! I had forgotten that. To be sure there must be one," said Florence, thoughtfully.

"Yes, 'my loss is his gain,' as old women say at what Gazettes call 'casualties.'"

"I do declare," cried Rosa, "'tis of more consequence to us than even to papa, what sort of man the new one is to be. I wonder whether he has thought of anybody."

"One comfort is, he won't live in the house, will he, as you have done? So we shall not depend so much upon his good nature and good humour as we have on yours?" asked Florence.

"I am sure I don't know. The house is big enough; and his Excellency must have a military sub at hand, to fetch and carry—to say nothing of your insisting upon all the delicate attentions I've inured you to. I should think they'll put him into my quarters here when once appointed."

"Oh, dear! oh, dear! that *will* be dreadful, if he isn't nice," said Rosa, much discomfited.

"Well, the young man has something in him, to my mind; though I doubt your finding him much of a 'squire for dames.'"

"So you know him, you tiresome!" cried both in a breath. "How dare you keep us in suspense in this way, then?"

"Official secrets are inviolable. Neither caress nor cruelty can wring one from me. Surely you know me well enough for that."

"Yes, well enough to know you wouldn't have said so much, if not free to say more; so give us his name forthwith."

"Flo knows it. I saw her dancing last night with its owner."

"You know very well she danced with half the garrison; to say nothing of the civil servants."

"Ah, but she couldn't dance the last quadrille with more than one partner at a time, could she?"

"Oh, then, Florence, there is a fate in it. It's Mr. Lockery, your solemn griff, you know."

"Locksley, my dear, Locksley—Ned Locksley the fellows call him; but neither of *you* shall call him Ned, for that's not proper; and I shall direct her Excellency's attention to the point before he joins."

"Don't be absurd, Willie. But tell us how papa can take so young an officer. He is only a griff, is he?"

"His Excellency, my venerable uncle, muttered something about obliging friends at home, my dear. Promotion by merit is at an end, you know, on *my* retirement. In fact, the thing's a job. Nevertheless, the lad is a likely lad."

"Well, tell us all about him. I'm dying to hear," said Rosa.

"What all about him? His looks, and manners, and aptitude for the 'valse à deux temps?' Florence can do the description a long chalk better than I can."

"How dare you," answered Florence. "No, but tell us what makes you think him a likely lad."

"'The cut of his jib,' I should say, but for professional prejudice against all nautical terms."

"Is that all?"

"Perhaps, not quite."

"What more, then?"

"Well, first and foremost, he is a desperate

student of 'the languages.' You know that's a hobby of mine: 'if you're to rule a nigger, speak as sich.' Them's my sentiments."

Rosa laughed, and clapped her pretty little white hands at his utterance of the ugly word, with an arch look at Florence.

"For shame, Willie!" said that young lady. "You know you have taken noble pains to win the confidence of natives by your knowledge of native languages and laws. And now you make a mock of your own nobleness, and encourage Rosa in her follies."

There was emotion in her voice, and it apparently moved Willie, for he said in a very different tone from any he had used—

"Thank you, Flo, for your good word, at any rate."

Rosa, put out for a moment, soon rallied, and said:

"I understand, then, Mr. Locksley will ask Flo to dance in Hindustani, offer ices in Urdoo, and thank her in Tamil for the honour of having held her fan. That, so far, is certainly satisfactory. What more?"

"He can ride a bit?"

"So can our black grooms, the Syces."

"Ah, but your Syces can't break that Arab your father bought from the Habesh horse-dealer for you, three weeks ago. Not one of them has ventured to mount him yet. Now, Locksley will do it, if it's to be done, I think."

"What makes you think so?"

"Because he has backed Major Brown's big chestnut, and jumped him over an awkward place, into the bargain. I saw him do it, and very neat it was, too. Perfect temper and iron nerve!"

"I never saw Major Brown's big chestnut."

"No, that's not the kind of nag for dress parade, nor evening promenade with fair equestrians. He is the most vicious brute in all Bombay; but I don't know that there's a charger in the garrison his match for speed and power."

"And what made Mr. Locksley mount him?"

"If Florence won't say that I am turning horse-jockey, like Stubbs of the Nizam, whom she stigmatized as such once in my hearing, you shall have the story."

"You seem sensitive of her highness's strictures, Willie. I did not know that was a weakness of yours."

"We all have our failings. May I go ahead, Flo?"

His cousin gave him a nod and pleasant smile.

"Well, there was some horse talk, if the truth be told, one evening at the mess of the 'Europeans.' That's his corps, you know. Being out of ear-shot of Miss Flo, I think I took some part in it, having a small turn that way, spite of her disapproval. There is a certain nullah; you know what that is, don't you?"

"Yes; a water-course, ravine, or some such thing, I think."

"Just so. There was a certain nullah then, about five miles off, which had stopped the whole field after a jackal one day. A dispute arose as to the power of any Arab to clear it in his stride. A thorough-bred English hunter, thoroughly broken, would do it; but whether an Indian-trained Arab would was questioned. There was a pasty-faced lad there of the name of Mansfield, belonging to some cavalry corps, I think, who was loud and noisy in the negative, calling upon any one to name a horse in the garrison that could clear the leap. Young Locksley, who had hitherto said nothing, named the Major's big chestnut, which convinced us all, at once, that he knew something of the shape a horse should have at his hind-quarter.

Mansfield laughed at him, rudely enough, asking

him what *he* knew about horses, and adding that he had never yet had the pleasure to see him even astride of a pony. Locksley, not a morsel put out, said he didn't know much about horses, but still thought the chestnut could clear the nullah. I must tell you, by the way, that Locksley is about the only sub in his corps who doesn't keep a horse or two, but lives in what other griffs call a queer 'close-shaving manner' altogether."

"Perhaps he is poor," suggested Florence, charitably, "and wants to keep within his income; a rule of life but little followed by his brother subs, I fear."

"No, they say his governor's well off enough; but that's neither here nor there. Mansfield seemed to think he'd got him in a corner, and asked him at last, outright, whether he meant to say that he wouldn't funk to ride the chestnut at the nullah himself.

"'I don't think that I should,' he answered very quietly.

"'Bet you, you don't do it!' the other cried. He didn't answer.

"'Bet you ten to one, you don't!' Silent still.

"'Bet you fifty to one!' No answer yet.

" 'I dare you to do it!'

"Locksley stood up with face on fire, about to speak, when a sudden recollection seemed to strike him, and with one effort he sat down again, saying—'Just as you please then.' Brown didn't know what to make of it. 'He don't look like a fellow to show the white feather, does he?' he asked of me, when we left the mess-room that evening. I said, 'more t'other'—an elegant expression I learnt from Florence."

"This is immensely interesting," Rosa said. "Go on, Willie, because you said you saw him take the leap."

"Why, yes, most unexpectedly. Brown couldn't get the thing out of his head, so he asked Locksley one morning whether he would like a mount for an early canter before breakfast.

" 'Of all things,' quoth he.

" 'Like to try the chestnut? He's a rum customer.'

" 'He's a very fine horse, Major. I wish I could afford to keep one; I would make a bid for him.'

" 'Ah well! Wait till you've had a ride on him or so.'

"But if the Major counted upon seeing his

griffin spilt, he was mistaken. 'Abool-Harg,' the 'father of heat,' as they call the chestnut, had got a cool rider, who sat him to perfection. The Major, who is rather shy of riding him himself begged of Locksley to give him his morning gallops any day, so he and Brown and I had several rides together. One day we neared the nullah.

" 'Any objection, Major?'

" 'Oh dear no; but it's a nasty place, sir.'

"So Locksley put the nag into a canter, and then a gallop, holding him well in hand for all the brute's tearing excitement. And over the nullah he took him as clean as a whistle, Brown and I craning piteously on the wrong side of it. What's more, he brought him back. So you see, young ladies, I was justified in stating that he could ride a bit."

"Why wouldn't he take up the other man's challenge, then?"

"Ah, Miss Rosey, you are just as curious as I was. For the life of me I couldn't help asking him."

"And he said?"—

" 'Just because it *was* a challenge.' 'Taken up one too many, perhaps,' said I. Whereat he smiled, and tickled the chestnut's ears, and set him plunging to distraction. What do you think of that, Miss Flo?"

"What you said you did, that he is a likely lad."

"Always the case with ladies. Turn up their nose at horse-jockeys, and let themselves be 'witched with noble horsemanship!' "

"I don't care for his horsemanship."

"For what then?"

"For his riding his own temper with the curb as well as the chestnut."

"Catch Flo tripping in her moral highjinks if you can, Master Willie," laughed his younger cousin. "But I like him for the leap!"

"To be sure you do. And so does Florence, who has the pluck of a fighting-cock in her, for all her prudence and propriety. But I'll tell you what it is now: you are not to spoil this youngster when you have got him here—neither with giddy good-nature, Miss Rosey; nor with grave good-nature, Miss Flo. Should merit get up in the market, there can be no doubt I may be back as commander-in-chief before long, and shall want him on my staff instead of your distaff—there now!"

With that he got up, and assuring them that

the public business of the Presidency was at a stand-still during his absence from his office, departed, deferring till evening his final leave-taking.

CHAPTER III.

"So you have actually appointed an aide-de-camp without consulting us! Is not that going a little too far, pappy dear?" asked Rosa, saucily. "Governors have a right to govern—to a certain extent; but there *are* limits."

"Rosa!" admonished her mother.

But Buffer Barrington—I crave his Excellency's pardon, the Right Honourable Frederick Barrington, C.B., and so forth—smiled, as a man will, at a dear daughter's playful waywardness, of whose dutifulness and love his heart need make no doubt. His Excellency was a trifle pompous at times even with her Excellency in person; but with his pet, Rosa, never.

"Don't cry till you are hurt, pussie; the aide-de-camp is not appointed yet."

"No; but the appointment is offered, and, if accepted, Florence and I can hardly cancel it."

"Speak for yourself, Miss Rosey," cried her cousin, "I am all for autocracy under his Excellency's administration."

"There, pussie! Niece more dutiful than daughter. What a lesson for you? Florence, your sentiments are exemplary."

"Oh dear, yes, when your Excellency's acts chance to meet her approval, her Queenship is all obedience. Offer the appointment to some officer under her sovereign displeasure—to Captain Stubbs of the Irregulars, for instance, and see her submission!"

"Am I to understand then," asked the Governor, much amused, "that the offer I have made is sanctioned by Miss Florence Barrington?"

"Certainly," said Rosa.

"I was not aware that either of you knew young Locksley, much less that Florence had distinguished him from other youngsters."

"Indeed uncle," answered Florence, "Rosa's nonsense passes those limits of which she was speaking. I should not presume to canvass an act of yours in any case; and as to Mr. Locksley, he was introduced to me the other night for the first time."

"And made a favourable first impression, eh? That goes a long way sometimes."

Rosa laughed; but Florence answered her uncle again without discomfiture.

"He is young for such an appointment, yet he struck me as older than his years."

"But, pappy dear," insisted Rosa, "do tell us what made *you* distinguish him, whether Queen Florence has or not?"

"I have caused inquiries to be made, Rosa, which, I am bound to say, result in allowing me to entertain the highest anticipations of this young gentleman's ability and character." His Excellency's style had suddenly grown official and full-mouthed. Miss Rosa was not to be put off so.

"Yes, dear pappy, but your inquiries don't satisfy mine. What made you make any about a griffin and a stranger, eh?"

"Well, the fact is, that Lord Royston, the Under-Secretary of State, a sort of cousin of ours you know, incidentally mentioned"——

Rosa laughed aloud; even Florence caught the infection. His Excellency reddened slightly.

"Don't be vexed with us, dear pappy," cried his daughter, putting her arms round his neck and her cheek to his; "it's not at you we are laughing—

that is, not exactly; but at that absurd Willie. Is not that true, Florence?"

"Pray what did Willie say to make you laugh, not exactly at me, young ladies?"

"He said promotion by merit ended with him, I think; and that his successor's appointment was in fact"——

"Was in fact what?"

"I think he said—a job."

"Monstrous impertinent of Master Willie!" bounced out his Excellency. But Rosa kept kissing and fondling him, so that his wrath should not get up real steam.

"Willie was only in fun, dear—you know his ridiculous way. He really thought you had done, as you always do, a wise thing in offering this to Mr. Locksley. He said he was a 'very likely lad,' and entertained us at length with his accomplishments. Didn't he, Flo? Tell this incredulous pappy what he said; he will believe you."

Thus invoked, Florence assured her uncle that Willie Sangster had spoken highly of the young officer in question.

"Praise from him is worth something you must admit, uncle."

"You are right about that, Florence. Greater

men than our griff might be proud of Willie Sangster's word."

"There, he's a dear, good, tame pappy now again, not a tiger and a tyrant any more," said incorrigible Rosey, with one or two additional kisses on his forehead.

She had but just returned to her own seat, when an Indian servant, gorgeous and picturesque as an illustrated edition of the Arabian Nights, brought a note to His Excellency, Sahib, with profound salaam.

"Wonders will never cease," he exclaimed, upon reading: "our young gentleman refuses."

"What young gentleman?"

"Young Locksley to be sure. He humbly solicits my Excellency's permission to decline the undeserved and unexpected honour proposed, and to remain my Excellency's obliged and obedient servant, &c. What do you think of that, young ladies?"

"Think of it! Think it's downright rude to us, your Excellency," cried Rosa, "whatever it may be to you."

"Perhaps Florence frightened him. She can put on an awful stateliness at times."

Rosa clapped her hands after her own fashion.

"Depend upon it, pappy dear, you have hit the

right nail on the head. Be candid with his Excellency, Flo. Did or did you not own, that on first introduction this admirable Crichton flinched from you?"

"Nonsense, Rosa!"

"Tell the truth, Miss Flo," said her uncle, with mock gravity. "Did you own he flinched, eh?"

Florence blushed crimson; but as she was one who never flinched herself, she answered:

"I said I thought his eyes did, for a second: perhaps it was all my fancy."

"O ho!" cried Barrington, in the same tone still, "this must be looked into. I cannot allow myself to be sneered out of my right of selection by Master Willie Sangster's impudence, nor this deserving young officer to be frowned out of his promotion by flashes from Florence's fine eyes, I can assure you. I have no time to investigate the matter this afternoon; but her Excellency shall issue her commands for his attendance at dinner this evening, and we will try to fathom the secret of his refusal before accepting it as final. Mind you girls are on your best behaviour."

The summons to Government House took Ned by surprise almost as much as the offered appointment. His Excellency had hinted nothing of his reasons for offering that, and Ned knew of none for his special invitation from the Governor's wife. He had arrived in India some time after the Barringtons, and it was true that he led, as Sangster had told the young ladies, an unusually retired and frugal life. When off duty he was absorbed in the studies begun under the old Major at Chatterham. Sangster he knew from having ridden out with him and Major Brown; but until Milward had introduced him to Florence Barrington he had no personal acquaintance with any other of their party.

The officers of the "Europeans" had received a collective invitation to the Governor's ball: Ned, individually, had availed himself of it to get sight and speech of that little pig's-eyed Ghoorka, whose shawls had attracted the attention of the Misses Barrington. He had determined to lose no opportunity, from the very first, of familiarizing himself with the appearance, manners, and dialects of the varied races which throng the wide empire ruled or overshadowed by the great anomalous Company whose commission he held. His only hesitation in declining the unexpected offer of promotion, arose from the thought that such opportunities would be multiplied and enlarged by accepting it. He had a good "think" over it, as in his happy, boyish days at Cransdale, the result of which had been what the Governor had announced. No such "think" was needed, however, over the sudden invitation to his Excellency's table. At the appointed hour Ned appeared in the unmitigated misery of full regimentals.

The Right Honourable F. Barrington, spite of his pomposity, was a kindly and thorough gentleman. His first few formal sentences set the young man at ease about the reception accorded to his refusal, though they might have shaken his determination to abide by it. For they gave him to understand that the appointment was still open to him, and almost condescended to apologize for the abruptness of the offer.

"I am aware, my dear sir, that in forming an almost personal relation such as this, there should be mutual acquaintance with character and disposition. Circumstances had not allowed me hitherto to afford you any fair opportunity for becoming acquainted with us. Captain Sangster's recall to his own Presidency came on us unexpectedly. On my own part, however, I should explain that I was naturally more than satisfied, from the circumstance that my cousin"——

But the nature of that circumstance and the

name of that cousin remained as yet unrevealed to Ned. The Ghoorka chieftain, brilliant with tremulous diamonds as a bristly boar with dew-drops from the jungle at morning, was ushered in, having a British staff-officer in attendance as interpreter. Exalted courtesies must pass between him and his Excellency, whereat the modest griffin bowed himself into the background amongst the ladies. But there his self-composure was forthwith to be tested more severely than in previous interview with the supreme authorities. For the quiet queenliness of Florence's gaze met him, and the brighter, quicker, if less penetrating, inquisition of Miss Rosa's.

"I think you said you knew Mr. Locksley, Florence; pray do me the favour to introduce him to me formally."

"Mr. Locksley; Miss Barrington, his Excellency's daughter, as I dare say Mr. Locksley knows."

"There," said that young lady, "we have observed the formalities. Not even a master of the ceremonies could object to our dismissing them now. We are very glad to make your acquaintance, Mr. Locksley. We know all about you from my first cousin, Willie Sangster."

"Indeed," said Ned, with a bow, not knowing

very well what to say. "It is very kind of him to have mentioned my name to you."

Could this possibly be the cousin to whom his Excellency had alluded? Could his cantering acquaintance with the late aide-de-camp give the clue to the surprising offer? Confidence is acquired on easy terms in India, should that be so.

As if in answer to these very questionings, Rosa went on:

"Yes, he told us all about the vicious chestnut, Abool Harg, was it not? and about the leap over the nullah."

Ned's modest confusion grew, and this time he said nothing, as he bowed again.

Perhaps "Buffer Barrington" had been a sporting county magnate at home in England, and would have a young soldier win his first spurs at an ugly jump. He didn't look much like a man for a flying leap, as he stood there to receive salaaming from the Ghoorka; but official grandeurs alter a man's bearing irresistibly.

"Even my cousin Florence here, who is a very stately lady, as you must have seen already, was interested in the story: and I was immensely."

Exactly so. Evidently an inherited taste. Her

father must have been a county centaur in slimmer days.

Willie Sangster's opinion of his seat on horseback must have suggested his name as his own successor.

"What's more, he made a promise for you, on the strength of your good horsemanship."

"No; did he, really?"

"Yes; papa has bought me the loveliest little Arab, of an Abyssinian dealer, from Hadramaut or some such place; but our Syces can't make him rideable for a lady. At least papa won't let me mount him yet; though I don't think I should be much afraid. Willie said you would break him in for me when you came here as aide-de-camp; but that is at an end, since you refuse to come."

"Come or not, Miss Barrington, I will redeem Captain Sangster's pledge, if you will honour me with a commission as roughrider. A true name often; but always a bad. Riding should never be rough. When it is, it ruins nine spirited horses out of ten. Ride your own temper and you can ride your horse."

"We know that *you* do *that*. Willie said so; and Florence said she admired you for it."

"Rosa dear, you are really—"

"Will you give your arm to my niece," interrupted her Excellency; Rosa having fallen, by virtue of her greater nearness to the throne, to the lot of the more dignified staff-officer, "the Himalayan bear-leader" as she afterwards irreverently called him.

"Do tell me," she said, "will they bring his Highness a live kid to tear at table? How dreadful! His mustachios are exactly like a tiger's whiskers. He looks so savage. I should not like to trust him with a knife myself; but I see he has a crooked dagger in his shawl, so that even taking the knife away wouldn't save the poor butler's life, should the chief take offence at any thing."

"If you should come here, after all, as my uncle's aide-de-camp, Mr. Locksley, you will have allowances to make for many random speeches of my lively cousin."

"Most men might think the risk of having such to make inducement enough to expose themselves to it."

"Whereas you refuse to run it? Is that your reason?"

Something made Ned look full at her; yet in the fulness of the look she thought she could perceive the shrinking which she had noted in his eyes at first. There was no fear in it, but an expression of regret or pain.

"I wonder if you would think me rude for telling you the truth?"

"I can never endure to be told any thing but that by any body."

Her tone again seemed to convey a summons that he should look straight at her and answer. As he did so, the shrinking and its sorrowfulness were seen by her, so as to be doubted of no more.

"I had quite forgotten, when I answered his Excellency's note, that the duties of an aide-de-camp in this house must of course place him in constant nearness to yourself and your cousin."

"And now that you remember it, are you shaken or strengthened, in your resolution?"

"Strengthened," he said, after a moment's pause. The sigh, which he suppressed, did not escape the ear of his fair questioner. She was at a loss to interpret it.

To repress her own curiosity would be, she felt, an easy task, compared with putting a check upon her cousin's. Perhaps it might be better and even braver, now they had once stepped upon confidential ground, to ask him outright, what otherwise Rosa would be sure to ask, his reasons for refusing her uncle's offer. He told her they were two, the expense and the occupation. After this she did not like to press him; but he took heart of grace himself, and said:

"You think, perhaps, such reasons want explaining. I own there is something of a paradox about the first; for an aide-de-camp's place carries some increase of pay, and he lives here at free quarters."

"Cousin Willie did, I know; and said he was getting as rich as Crœsus."

"Yes; but I should have to change my manner of life altogether, and incur some expenses at least, which I cannot well afford. Since you have been kind enough to question me, Miss Barrington, I will be honest and own that I am in debt."

"Already?"

"Oh! you are Indian enough to know how common that is, are you, Miss Barrington? I hope my confession will not quite lose me in your opinion."

"Not quite; next to the courage of not committing a fault comes that of repairing it at any cost."

"It is just of my determination to do that, that I wish to convince my creditor, who has the noblest heart in the world, Miss Barrington, and would never ask me for a farthing."

"All the more reason to satisfy him to the uttermost. I am sure you are quite right there."

"Thank you. I am equally sure that your approval is worthy encouragement." She felt the same longing regretful look steal into his eyes, and fix on her. She determined to go through with it.

"I think, you said, the occupation deterred you too. My uncle is not a 'roi fainéant,' every one allows; but I feel certain, that is, I should imagine —I mean—I gathered from what cousin Willie said, that you were not an idler even in this idle atmosphere."

"It is not the work, but the nature of it that I fear."

"Afraid of having to dance attendance upon her Excellency and the young ladies? I *have* heard aide-de-camp's duty so defined. But that is not what my uncle expects of his—neither do *we* expect it, Mr. Locksley. Since you knew my cousin, you must have known that he was not an officer of that stamp," she insisted, almost offended.

"Florence is queening it over that luckless young man," said Rosa, directing the "bear-leader's" attention to them across the table. "Does she not look grand with that expression? He is a bold boy not to wince under it."

For she could not see, as Florence still saw, what swam as if behind the pupils of his eyes.

"Captain Sangster's name is enough in India to tell even such a griff as I," said Ned, "that there is something else to be done here besides dangling or dancing attendance on any one."

"Why refuse, then, to follow him in his occupation?"

"Because I am not yet fit as he was to do desultory work without becoming less fit for work of any kind. He is a consummate Indian linguist, and an accomplished engineer. I was an English schoolboy last year, and am only an Indian recruit this."

"Wouldn't your position with my uncle give you many opportunities?"

"Which, as I now am, I fear I could only waste."

Struck with respect for his purpose of self-culture and self-control, Florence felt that she could pursue the personal question no further; yet she would not let the conversation jolt out of the groove in which it had been set running. She was sure of having found a sympathiser in what her saucy cousin called her "Eastern heroics," and spoke with spirit and enthusiasm of that great map of human interests which Hindostan unrolls to sight of any thoughtful, generous mind.

She understood as she did so that her new friend's spirit went stride for stride with hers, not at adventure, but as if on familiar ground. What she still could not explain, even in conjecture, was the wistful retrospective expression of his look, so manful and so strong.

"She'll turn that ensign's brain or drive him melancholy mad before the evening is out," again said Rosa, who now perceived the double play of feeling on Ned's features. "I wish mamma would give the signal and release him. You would be quit of my chattering, too, colonel, to your great relief."

Whilst the staff-officer was yet endeavouring to convince her of the irreparable loss he should sustain by her departure to the drawing-room, her Excellency gave the expected nod of female masonry, and the Ghoorka's little eyes stared, strangely wide for them, at the sudden rising and retreat of the ladies.

"Well, Florence," began her cousin, the instant they came together, "that young gentleman withdraws his refusal I can see."

"Maintains it, you mean, Miss Rosey."

"Withdraws it."

"We shall see."

"We shall."

But Miss Rosa's intention of exploring Ned's forthwith was frustrated on the first return of the gentlemen from the dining-room. Young Locksley seemed to have struck up a sudden acquaintance with the polyglot staff-officer, and they were in deep conversation. This was followed up by a presentation to the ugly little glittering chief. All Ned's attention seemed given to him and to the talk which he made through the interpreter to the group of officials and others who gathered around him. Vainly did Rosa watch for so much as one glance, not towards herself—she did not expect one—but towards her cousin. This was provoking. Some hint, however, was apparently given by his Excellency the Governor that he wished for more significant and less public discourse with the hillman chief, for the group broke up and fell away, leaving the three high discoursing parties to themselves.

Perverse fate in the person of Captain Stubbs of the Irregulars, who had dropped in to pay his devoirs at the sort of evening levee perpetually held, again interfered with her design of boldly summoning the ensign to an interrogatory. Nevertheless, to her great consolation under this infliction, she presently descried that some law of gravitation had once more brought Ned to the side of Florence. Stubbs was tenacious, and in his way as audacious as the young lady in hers. Hints he would not take, and met what might count as direct dismissal from further attendance with something very like defiance. But Rosa beat him off at last, and, like a saucy steam-tug bearing down on two consort barques, darted into their conversation. The effect upon one of them could not have been much more startling had she been a gun-boat firing live shell into the craft she purposed to take in tow.

"Oh, Mr. Locksley, tell me, do you know Lady Constance Cranleigh, Lady Cransdale's daughter? I dare say you do."

Poor Ned! Never thereafter on the soil of India did the first crash of ringing musketry nor the deep breach of silence by the roar of sudden artillery make his nerves quiver as did those unexpected words from the light-hearted girl, who was not looking at him, but at the ludicrously profound obeisance of the chief taking leave of her father. Even Florence saw little on his countenance of what effort it cost him to say—

"I know Lady Cransdale and her family very well."

"I thought you must, because Lord Royston knows you. He wrote about you to papa."

Ned could say nothing, between rage at a recommendation from that quarter and suppressed exultation at having refused the offer it had brought him.

"I never saw Lady Constance, but have been told there's a great likeness between her and my cousin here. That's what made me ask you. Do *you* think there is?"

Florence remembered afterwards—at least, she felt sure it had been so—how, without lifting his eyes to her face for a momentary comparison, without a momentary pause to call up an image to his memory, he had answered in a hurried way—

"A singular likeness; I saw it at first."

"I suppose it is no news to tell you of their engagement?"

"Whose?"

"Lord Royston's and Lady Constance's. It is announced in London. Mamma heard by the mail to-day. They are to be married soon."

"I have not had letters," he contrived to mutter.

"Oh, I dare say you will when they are sorted. Ours are brought in papa's special bag."

"Excuse me, then," he said, with tremulous accent, "my letters may be at my quarters by this time. One longs for a line from home. Good night!"

CHAPTER IV.

His mother's letter confirmed Rosa Barrington's news, almost in as few words as hers.

Yet news it was not, nor needing any confirmation? Had not he known it, and for certain, long ago? What else had turned the current of his life and brought him here, so far from home, alone?

He looked out at his open window, upwards: the silver splendour, of which the blue night air was full, brought back the moonlit summer-night at Freshet to his mind. He let his glance droop downwards; there was no dancing plain of wavelets across which fancy might sail into boundless distances of hope.

A barrack wall rose up before him blank and high, inlaid, however, with dark shadows from trees of foreign foliage in the courtyard, spiky fronds of palm, and broad blades of banana, let in, as it were in ebony, on the white chunam of the wall.

An English sound came ringing through the night. Not a long cheery hail from a boatman in the bay; but the sharp challenge of an European sentry, followed by the rattle of presented arms.

What, indeed, had brought him here? Had he not known it, and for certain, long ago?

Stern and bitter, and new to young men, is the difference between what only may be and what is. Yet happier and more hopeful—for all it seem to them so hopeless—than the difference, in which their elders' souls are schooled, between what is and that which might have been.

Were they the pariah dogs, or distant troops of jackals, which kept up such dismal howlings? Can the jar upon the ears' nerves bring moisture into the eyes? Or what else dims and blurs the lines of Lucy's clear fine penmanship before her son's eyes? They must be jackals howling; for they are scouring away miles off now: all is so still again as their noise dies out. But no sound pierces after all like the scream which a bird will fling down from her winged height of soaring. That must have been a bird's scream! Ned recalled the clang of the sea-mew on whose breast he had seemed to discern the bloodspot as he lay staring skywards. Ah, how hot the sun was there! But the breeze was fresh and cool. So different from these sultry nights in India! He threw himself back upon his barrack bed, as he had done upon the crisp turf at the Skerry. By-and-by he fell asleep.

But the musquito is a wakeful fly.

Rising feverish and excited more than jaded at morning, it was a relief to hear a hubbub outside.

There must be some mistake about it, a native servant was insisting. Locksley Sahib did not please to keep horses, and seldom rode out except with Major Brown.

Then was heard plunging, and squealing, and the scattering of gravel or small stones.

Then imprecations and entreaties, according to diverse formularies, Mussulman and Hindoo.

Then asseverations from attendant Syces, for there seemed to be a bevy of them, that no mistake existed or could exist, for Missy Khanum herself had sent them, and, proof unimpeachable, here was a "chit" from her for Locksley Sahib.

Why couldn't this father-in-law of donkeys have stated that before?

Plungings, squeals, and scattering noise again. And loud repudiation, with retorts, of the unseemly epithets: until the appearance of Ned himself restored something like a semblance of discipline and order.

The "chit" was, of course, a note from Rosa, written over night, to say she took him at his word about her Arab, and sent him therewith for immediate experiment.

Nothing could have pleased him better than the necessity for making it. He would find vent for the excitement which was on him, whilst forced to put constraint upon himself, and on the wrathfulness which, to his shame and vexation, had been roused within him.

The mere mounting would have been an uneasy task for many men; the keeping of the skilfully-won seat uneasier; the coaxing and compelling of the creature first out of the enclosure, then along the road, uneasiest of all.

As the horse was suffered to break into a gallop, and disappeared in a cloud of dust, a one-eyed sowar of Stubb's Irregulars turned to the nearest Syce, and asked to what cavalry corps that young officer belonged.

"To none," he answered, "to these European Fusiliers."

"Koompni Bahawdur is a fool then," said the

sowar. "What son of a burnt father expects such a rider as that to walk afoot? He's the man to head a rissalah of horse!"

"And you would like to ride rissaldar under him, eh, Nusr-ed-deen?" asked a bystander.

"Inshallah!" quoth the trooper, "I shall keep my one eye on him; who knows but I may?"

But the Syces prophesied that before the morning was out some peasant would pick the rider up out of a ditch with broken leg or arm. Lucky for him if it should not be his neck bone.

Whereat the sowar laughed in scorn, and turned on his heel, with an extra twirl to his grizzled mustachios.

He was the truer prophet. Had it been otherwise, Ned would not have been able to wield his pen and write home thus to Lucy Locksley—

"Dearest Mother,

"Thank God for the good account of yourself and my dear father. Thank you for all the other items of home news; short time as one has been gone, one hungers for them as if that time were as wide as the space which parts us now. I know you will not think me selfish; perhaps not even—how I hate the word—sentimental, for owning at once that one short sentence in your letter stood out to my eyes in different relief and character from all the rest. I need not tell you which. How glad I shall be to hear of the marriage having now taken place! I shall be then face to face with fact, not with possibility, however seemingly unavoidable its event. Don't think me such a fool as to have been speculating upon any wild improbabilities; but fool or no fool, one cannot feel quite the same towards what has not yet befallen and what has. A whole world of fact and duty will separate between a Lady Constance and a Lady Royston. As for ignoring fact, or flinching from duty, I will, my life long, God helping, never do either.

"You tell me to be sure and fill my letters with all that concerns myself around or within. I should almost fear that was an exhortation to egotism, were it not that I know the self-devotion of the dear mother's heart from which it springs. As for what is around me, now that the first novelties which I tried to describe to you have worn old—all was dull and monotonous enough till within the last few days. Even drill and parade had dwindled into repose and inactivity, under the increasing heat. The best mechanism for punkahs and 'thermantidotes,' a sort of magnified and modified bellows in use out here, was absorbing one's thoughts and conversation, till *my* mind, at least, got a shock of surprise. I received an offer from the Governor, the Hon. F. Barrington, to appoint me his own aide-de-camp. Vanity whispered that merit was soon appreciated upon Indian ground. But as my chief reputation is for stinginess, 'sapping'—you know what that is—and a little horse breaking, I wondered much which feature in it could have conciliated his Excellency. For the stinginess, I have my reasons, which in due time shall appear to you, dear mammy. The 'sapping' will have your approval, I know. And for the horse breaking; don't you be anxious about my going 'on the turf,' dear, the less as there is, alas! under this fierce sun, no turf to go upon. What's more, my stinginess extends to not even keeping what is out here called a 'tat;' but at home a pony. My mention of these three reputed characteristics of mine, I beg leave to say, bears directly upon the matter in hand. Horses, smart clothes, and additional servants would, I thought, be necessary if I were to accept; and my studies would suffer interruption. So I declined, with thanks, little thinking how matters really stood. I was then asked to dine at Government House, and learnt to my terrible disturbance, that Lord Royston's good offices had brought my name into notice there. I am ashamed to the quick, to-day, to think of the scornful hot and sour resentment which boiled up within me at this announcement. It is humiliating beyond expression to find one has made so little way towards the conquest of one's méaner self!

"But that is not all I have to tell you. The Governor has a daughter and a niece out with him. To the latter, I had been introduced, some day or two before, and judge of my surprise in recognising in her, at first sight, the strangest likeness to Lady Constance Cranleigh!

"Strange likeness, yet I need hardly tell you how imperfect and how inferior. There is something of the royalty of Lady Constance's expression in that of Miss Florence Barrington; but its ineffable sweetness and winsome repose are wanting. She has a fine figure; but without that exquisite proportion and nameless grace—ah! mother dear, I must not trust myself to write this way. There is considerable affinity, besides, between their minds. I had much conversation with her last evening when I dined there; for I sat beside her. It was wonderful and almost unbearable, to look into a face so like the other's, and hear words so like what she might have spoken, uttered in a voice so unlike her own. You know the rich music of her's; there is not even a reminiscence of it in the tones of Florence Barrington.

"This young lady's likeness and unlikeness to Lady Constance, exercise on me, so far, a very see-saw of attraction and repulsion. Her presence under her uncle's roof would be an additional reason for declining the appointment, the offer of which he was kind enough to keep open still. I hope my firm determination is not stiffened into mere obstinacy by the introduction of Lord Royston's name; but I shall hardly feel sure of that, till I hear back from my father and yourself that you approve of it, on the grounds I stated at first. Political and military matters are all as drowsy here as the possible actors in them, at least the English portion of them. Tell Phil, when my father writes, that I envy him the soldierly stir and bustle of the barracks in Bird-cage Walk. Chatterham was a perfect whirl of strategical excitement compared to this, and Major Anderson a sort of Alexander beside the old general who commands this garrison. Our men feel the listlessness and monotony sadly. Too many take to the canteen, night, noon, and morning, on account of it. I am always in fear of Tommy Wilmot, sober and steady as he is keeping hitherto. His active mind and body get less scope for their activity than even in the garden at the lodge. Don't tell his parents this; but say, which is the truth, that he is hitherto hearty and well. And now good bye for this mail. God bless you, dearest mother, and my own dear father too. You know that it is no mere form for me to write myself,

"Your most dutiful and loving

"NED."

Persisting in his refusal to act as the father's aide-de-camp, he had, perhaps inconsiderately, accepted the duties of equerry to the daughter. In virtue of which acceptance, Miss Rosa soon found means to make his frequent attendance upon herself and her cousin, almost a matter of regulation. Their Excellencies were at first a little inclined to resent his cavalier treatment of their official offer; but this Rosa would not allow, declaring that his offence against herself and Florence was far more presumptuous, and exhorting parental authorities to copy their superior magnanimity in over-looking it. As to mamma's suggestion, that without being implacable, there was no need to show him special attentions, which might possibly be misinterpreted, it was met by the undeniable argument that there could be no reasonable objection to having about the house one whom they had twice offered to take into it. And Florence, in the least obtrusive manner, contrived to convert her uncle to the belief that the apparently offensive refusal was an act of commendable prudence and modesty on the part of so young and inexperienced an officer. Further acquaintance increased the good will of both the cousins towards him. Rosa liked him for his equable temper, which her teasing could never put out; and was grateful for his success with her little Arab, which was soon complete. She was charmed, moreover, she declared, at finding "so civil a lad who never tendered any civilities, a liegeman who never bored her by proferring homage."

Florence divined the strong spirit which swept under the smooth humour, and took an almost dangerous delight in kindling the enthusiasm which underlay his quiet bearing.

His growing intimacy with the Governor's family could not escape the observation of his comrades. Some joked, some sneered at it. Milward was among the former, though he would not venture on the topic in Ned's presence, and claimed for himself the credit of having got him appointed "aide-de-camp to the young ladies."

Mansfield, true to the old Chatterham grudge, was among the latter; and catching up the phrase one day from Milward said, that "the young ladies' aide-de-camp was sneaking after an appointment as aide-de-camp to the old gentleman."

"Why sneaking, pray?"

"Because he is undermining Wilkinson, who got it after Sangster left."

"Who is that undermining Wilkinson?" asked Major Brown, a great friend of the last-named officer. He had only caught the last words of the speaker.

"Locksley, of the Europeans," answered Mansfield, somewhat against the grain, for he anticipated the rejoinder the Major did not fail to make.

"You put your foot in it about him once before, I mind, young gentleman, and you'll be doing it again, maybe, more seriously."

"Do you mean to say he hasn't an eye to Wilkinson's appointment?"

"Do you mean to say he has?"

"I do."

"Shows all you know about it, then. He refused it when it was offered him, before Wilkinson had a chance."

"That's all very well to say, Major."

"Do you doubt my word, young gentleman?" he cried, angrily.

"No; but your information. From who did you have it?"

"I don't know that I should tell you, if it wasn't to stop the mischief you might make, sir. The Governor told me so himself."

There was no answering this, so Mansfield muttered:

"Oh, then, I beg your pardon; but I think that Mr. Locksley is a regular humbug still."

"You'll find that hard to prove, I take it," said the Major.

Not a little hurt by the tone his senior had taken with him, Mansfield watched with the malicious narrowness of a mean mind's observation for any thing which might help to establish the proof to which the Major had challenged him. Some months, however, slipped away before he could seize on any thing which he thought he might safely venture to produce in detriment of Ned's good name.

There was a Mr. Campbell, a civilian, who dined not seldom at the mess of the Europeans, as also at that of the cavalry corps to which Mansfield himself belonged. He was an hospitable entertainer at his own, as well as a willing guest at other men's tables; and at his house Mansfield and Locksley, met, one day, together at dinner. A Mr. Mavor, one of the H.E.I.C.'s chaplains was also present. Some stir had been made recently among the English community upon the subject of missionary work in India; and by some means, half way through the dinner, the topic was started.

Mr. Campbell, a hard-headed man—of that class whose hardness of head approaches to the wooden; a practical man—of that variety whose practice is to cling in spite of any demonstration to their own favourite theories—was loud in repudiation of the idea that it was possible to convert a Hindoo, by conviction, to Christianity.

"Rice converts, in hard times, you may get a few. Ha! ha! ha! Excuse me, Mr. Mavor; but you know *you*'re not a missionary. Real converts, there never was one. Don't tell me, sir. I've known these niggers, men and boy, these twenty years and more."

The Company's chaplain, a quiet but firm-looking clergyman, waited till the guffaw of the host and certain of the guests subsided.

"As you have said, sir," he replied, "I cannot claim the honourable title of a missionary; but I have looked a little closer, perhaps, than you have felt bound to do into the work of missions here."

"Well, come now, Mr. Mavor," cried the civilian; "you're a straight-forward sort of man I know. Sink the professional; we're all among friends here. Did ever you know a converted nigger worth his salt?"

"Hear! hear!" went the laughers, Mansfield among the number.

"What sort of a man's your under-butler? Please don't mention his name, or look at him just yet. I mean the man behind Mr. Locksley's chair."

"Oh, he's a first-chop fellow for a native. What makes you want to know?"

"Never mind just yet, sir. Have you found him an honest man?"

"Honest enough. I trust him with any amount in silver or in gold. I suppose he makes his little perquisites, however, in the way of business, like the rest of them. Ha! ha!"

"But you never caught him even filching, or lying, or the like?"

"Never that I know of. What on earth are you driving at, my dear sir?"

"In fact you own him worth his salt?"

"Worth a wheelbarrowful. He's my best servant. I shall promote him when the old khansamah dies."

"Then I have answered your question. That man is a Christian?"

"The dickens he is! How came you to know that?"

"One whose conversion cost him house and home. You may take my word for it."

"Be hanged if I do! I say, Panjerah," cried his excited master, no longer in English, to the man, who stood motionless, with downcast eyes and arms folded, Easternwise, across his breast.

"What's all this Padre Sahib's nonsense? What's your caste, man? What's your religion? What poojah do you make, eh?"

Without shrinking, yet without affectation, the man raised his eyes: those of every man besides in company being full fixed on him.

"I am a Christian, sir!" he said, distinctly.

His master laughed again more scornfully.

"What did you get for turning from the padre?"

But Ned rose, with indignation, and turning to the Hindoo held out his hand.

"Do me the honour to take it!" and he seized

the slender, dark fingers in his own strong grip.

Much talk was made thereafter of his impulsive action: some praise. Mansfield was eager in comments to the disadvantage of the man whom he detested.

"Humbug or not, we hope you'll favour us with a candid opinion on it, Major Brown. You are not in the saintly line yourself, we know."

"I never owned it so much to my shame as now," he answered. "I only wish I had the heart in me with which he did it. I think him a finer fellow than I did before."

"That same is not aisy, Major, since his riverence rode yer chestnut at the lape!" laughed O'Brien, who would have his joke.

CHAPTER V.

It was a singular coincidence enough, that "good little Mr. Gossett," as Miss Davenant had called him, had been the late and, in due course, the present Lord Royston's man of business also. It was, perhaps, more singular, that amidst all the pressure of his extensive and confidential business, he should never have become "Gossett and Anybody-else." Even his head clerk had been pure clerical clerk, confidential in few but minor matters. It, therefore, was not singular at all that his death, occurring at that peculiar crisis in Lord Royston's history, which craves unusual attention to "settlements," should cause some little inconvenience to that rising statesman.

"I really wish, dear Mr. Locksley, you would

take pity on a poor bothered Under-sec, and act for me, or see that I'm acted for, just as you will for Lady Constance."

"That would look ugly, if any one hereafter should object to anything."

"Who on earth should? I don't want to make it a controversy, a plaintiff and defendant affair. I'm only anxious for what you are, to see that Lady Constance's interests are well secured if I should die, against greedy 'collaterals.'"

"I don't think it would do," said Robert Locksley, "for me to meddle with it, or instruct any one on your account. Men of business are plenty. Put yourself in the hands of some eminent and trusty firm: Pinkerton and Solway, for instance, or Blore, Sarsden, and Kimmeridge."

"Not a bit of it. Such legal leviathans terrify me. I want something safe and quiet, such as poor dear little old Gossett was himself."

"There is Mr. Fowler, my lord, at Cransmere."

"A good sort of man, I grant—but a leetle thick-headed, you must yourself allow."

"Wonder what your lordship would say to my trying a stroke of nepotism?"

"Nepotism! Why, my dear sir, it is the air we breathe in office, if I'm to believe the papers. Being a government official, I should own you as 'a man and a brother.' "

"Well, the fact is, my wife has a nephew."

"A lawyer? He's the man for me, then."

"He's very young, my lord."

"I am not a Methuselah myself, you know."

"He is not a bit like little Mr. Gossett."

"Perhaps he is like Mrs. Locksley, which is a deal better."

"He has an older head with him; who was under his late father; who certainly has a touch of the Gossett element."

"Name of the firm?"

"Burkitt and Goring."

"Direction?"

"Solicitors, Freshet."

"A thousand thanks, dear sir. That's one weight off my mind."

He booked the names and address in a small pocket-book, declaring that he would write that evening. He did; and so it befell that Burkitt and Goring acted for his lordship in the matter of marriage settlements. Keane had gained a footing at Rookenham. He spared no resource of tact or diligence to make it secure. His relation to the Locksleys made a powerful prejudice in his favour, and helped his endeavour to complete success. Without any apparent servility, he was so useful and obliging that Lord Royston was led on to consult him upon many matters not strictly connected with actual "settlements," yet, such as marriage-tide is a time for settling. He and his bride were to have a couple of months in Scotland, by the considerate kindness of the secretary under whom he served. Being tied, therefore, beforehand, closely to his official desk, there were endless things to be done at Rookenham, to which it was impossible that he should attend: these, Keane took off his hands in the easiest and most natural manner. Under such circumstances he was often over on business, of greater or less import, from Freshet; and as Cransdale was so near, dined and slept most evenings at the Lodge. The room next to Ned's, which Philip had occupied as a boy, came to be called Keane's. The connection between himself, his uncle, and his aunt, grew naturally closer and more confidential. Robert Locksley could not but be pleased with the interest he displayed in all matters which concerned the business of the Cransdale estate, and was secretly flattered by the intelligent approval his nephew bestowed on his own really masterly management. The key to Lucy's heart was in the hands of one, whose memory treasured with gratitude and esteem the image which absence only kept in more vivid continuance before her sight.

The companionship and conversation of two such charming relatives could not but exercise some influence upon Keane. It was not merely that he looked upon a picture of enduring faith and tenderness in family life; but that he breathed the very breath of its worth and sweetness, and felt in his heart's fibres its fruitful and delicious warmth. Yet human hearts, like more material substances, vary in their power of conducting, reflecting, or accumulating heat. His manner towards his mother improved under this influence with truer improvement than that wherewith his tact and self-control had lacquered it over in the actual presence of his aunt. Unconscious imitation of the kindly courtesy which coloured the common places of life at the Locksleys, wrought this change for the better. But his appreciation of her motherliness, of its true force and tenderness for him, suffered loss upon the whole. With the ready injustice of a selfish son's heart—injustice too ready, perhaps, in the heart of the least selfish son—he made comparisons between mother-love, as his own mother had shown it, and mother-love as he saw it pervade the feelings, thoughts and words—the very life—of Lucy.

Both had abundant overflow indeed: but one showed barren beside the other. Ungrateful! Nile waters gladden even the Nubian sand; but only where the Delta's deep loam drinks them do the oxen browse knee-deep in green succulence, tread, presently, knee-deep in harvest gold. Lucy and her sister-in-law had lavished love on different soils. Again he noted favourably the equable flow of Lucy's strong affection, remembering against his mother the capriciousness of hers. Amidst all her large indulgence, he bethought him, she had been sometimes harsh with him and even violent in years by-gone. Ungrateful again! Had not these old attempted severities expressed the widow's wish to gift his boyhood with the lost blessing of a father's irresistible authority? But her present uniform weak concession to his own will showed in pitiful contrast even with that old fitful energy. A coward shows sometimes worse even than a bully. Thrice ungrateful! Why fail thus to perceive in her submission to a son's manhood, the reassertion in her widowed heart of the woman's loving instinct to obey?

But Keane's domestication with the Locksleys wrought yet another effect upon him. His better selfishness was won to note with special interest the charm, so new to the inmate of a widow's home, which married companionship may give to common life. Dispassionate after a sort, and of forecasting mind, a stranger to the fanciful aspirations in which most young men at his age indulge, he was both struck and pleased, as few such would be, by the lesser, homelier delights wherewith he saw that Lucy smoothed her husband's daily course. He had spoken of his uncle's feathering his nest at Cransdale, using the metaphor in its most mercenary sense. Now he perceived a new sense in the figure, in which his imagination was well pleased to coozle and lie snug.

Golden guineas would build a tower of defence. Its thick walls and high battlements would make its owner powerful. But he began to think, as he had not thought before, of the soft and quiet comfort which might be likewise fitted up within. He was not haunted by a poet's dream of a "fair ladye's bower" within a castle-keep, but planned the design of a sitting-room which should be gracefully comfortable.

Fanny Davenant, however, it is not to be denied,

sat ever in a "causeuse" in this chamber of imagery. Whatever grace and tenderness familiarity with such imaginings wrought upon Keane's tone and manner, told upon the character of his intercourse with her. She could not fail to perceive, nor yet to be won upon by this mellowing and harmonizing change.

Unstudied and unartificial, it gave Keane an advantage, unsuspected at first by either. It seemed to supply the missing element in the quality of such homage as he had hitherto partly tendered for her acceptance, partly assumed a right to impose upon it. Leaving untouched his superiority over other competitors in the restricted arena of their local society, it suggested an abatement of his pretensions to supremacy over herself, and thus rendered less necessary the jealous assertion of her own power as against him. An heiress, moreover, even when unaware of her own vantage ground, becomes an object of real deference to such men as Keane Burkitt; and Fanny Davenant, knowing nothing of what caused his increased submissiveness, might pardonably attribute it to the deepening of his attachment and admiration. As Keane won upon her, so did she upon him. Becoming, by almost insensible degrees, less defiant, she was becoming more winsome to one in his present mood. If no fresh ardour were kindled, some new tenderness was instilled, the very element required to make the man appear both more loving and more loveworthy.

But all these developments were very gradual. Miss Davenant's will was not yet signed, and all uncertainties must counsel caution to well-regulated minds. Even had it been signed and sealed, Keane's sense of what is due to the authority of elders—perhaps his acquaintance with the effects of codicils—seemed to whisper that, before "committing" himself, it might be well to sound, on opportunity, the disposition of Fanny's aunt towards his suit. Should it prove hostile, not only would there be danger to the dowry, but his own legacy might go to the dogs—or rather to the cats. This was a delicate investigation, wherein precipitancy might be fatal. Nothing, therefore, could be more deliberate and unobtrusive than Keane's wooing. It found, however, in his own mother, an unsolicited auxiliary. She had at once perceived the softening of his manner with herself, and sunned her heart at first, in its new smiles, with unconcern, as the seamews on the Skerry preen their wings in the pale warmth of wintry suns, which can scarce yet be said to herald spring-time. But, pale warmth as it might be, it was marvellous pleasant; and when it seemed to keep on shining, unlike the gleam of those short, fitful breaks of winter, she began, with joy, to speculate on its continuance, and to seek about, in curious hope, for the source of the new light and warmth. Little by little her eyes were drawn to Fanny Davenant; they saw, what no one else saw, the imperceptible growth of intimacy between her and Keane. This discovery challenged gratitude by too good a claim to rouse in her the jealousy which the conquest of Ned's heart by Lady Constance had roused in Lucy. The mother, rich in possession of her son's love, had almost resented its first attachment elsewhere as a robbery. The mother, poor by doubt of her son's affection, hailed it as, perhaps, a promise of restoration.

Mrs. Burkitt's heart forthwith adopted Fanny Davenant. Fearful of seeming to have surprised a confidence which neither word nor look from her son had willingly given her, she carefully forbore to give him intimation that his secret was in her possession. Fearful also of injuring him with Fanny, should she give her reason to suspect that her suitor had brushed the bloom from off his suing, even by letting a mother's hand handle it, she was very guarded, as she thought, in her approaches to closer acquaintance with this adopted daughter of her heart. But Fanny was beginning to believe more and more in Keane's affection; she was beginning to suspect herself also more and more of returning it. Her interest, therefore, in what was his quickened her observation day by day, and an intuitive knowledge arose in her of the yearning of his mother's heart towards herself. The quiet, loving deference with which Mrs. Burkitt treated her produced a bashful, but not unpleasing confusion in her feelings. She could not but accept it as a pledge of the sincerity of the son's quiet attentions to her, and, accepting it as such, could not be wrong in finding a special sacredness and sweetness in its nature. There was a tacit understanding soon between the elder and the younger woman, the caressing atmosphere of which exercised upon the latter a very powerful influence. Keane, without suspecting its cause, perceived his mother's liking for the object of his own choice; and though her disapproval of his selection would not much have troubled him, he was glad enough to find that she gave it her unsolicited sanction. Home life was wonderfully sweetened thus, both for mother and son. Office life, at the same time, continued to be prosperous. At Keane's earnest solicitation, his own proceedings on behalf of his noble client, in the marriage settlements, had been submitted by Lord Royston to eminent conveyancing authorities in London, and a flattering verdict had been given upon the precision, clearness, and comprehensiveness of his work.

"It's no use doing things by halves, my dear Mr. Locksley," Lord Royston said, a few days previous to the wedding; "I shall have all the boxes of Rookenham deeds and documents, which little Gossett had, intrusted to your nephew before I leave. I've always been flattering myself with hopes of minding my own business; but it's not compatible with minding that of the State, even in my subordinate situation. Besides, I shall have a wife to look after now, and shall steal all possible spare time for her."

"No government is sempiternal," said the other, good humouredly; "nor many honeymoons, as I believe."

"Well, the Houses are up: so we are safe till February. I shan't shake off the cares of office till then: and even the shortest honeymoon will run up arrears of work for me. So my tin boxes must find their way to Freshet for a time at least. That needn't give your nephew a regular vested interest in them. If, hereafter, the base intrigues of faction should drive such a statesman as I from official occupation, they'll be nearer Rookenham than they are in town, and I can re-claim them."

Keane himself came up, therefore, to take formal charge of them, and so was present at the marriage.

It was celebrated in London, against the natural longings of Lady Cransdale and her daughter. But among other reasons which determined them to drive in bridal pomp to a town church portico, rather than walk on the moss to the chapel porch in Cransdale Park, was their consideration for Mrs. Locksley. At home, they would not have known whether to ask or to leave her uninvited. Her presence might have been irksome and painful to herself; her absence, when close at hand, within the ring-fence of the Park, would have been unnatural, depressing, and sorrowful to Lady Constance. As it was, there was a grand wedding, and Philip gave away the bride, with a paternal unction and gravity, for which Katey Kilmore, who was a bridesmaid, and wept profusely herself during the ceremony, laughed at him unmercifully in the less affecting atmosphere of the banquet-room. Even the immediate instructions touching his private affairs, which Keane had received from Lord Royston, were delayed to the last moment, hurried and incomplete. On one money matter, of some importance, the late Mr. Gossett's head clerk himself was as much at a loss as Keane; but referred him for elucidation to an eminent stockbroker who had intermeddled in the transaction.

Keane found this Mr. Sherbrooke a pleasant gentlemanly man, whose shrewdness and intelligence were mellowed by the good humour bred of prosperity. He was evidently a busy man, yet one who loved such ease and luxury as were not wholly incompatible with success in business.

"I am not quite sure," he said, "about that stock of Lord Royston's; but I will look through my memoranda. A trifle it was; I think, some four or five thousand only."

There were substantial men and money sums in Freshet affairs; but the unaffected magniloquence of this metropolitan estimate of trifles impressed the country man of business considerably.

"Let me see, now; three years ago, you say?" turning over a whole drawer full of metallic memorandum books. "Some time in August, was it, or earlier? I do believe it must be in that identical book I took down home last week, and forgot in my dressing-room. Do you stay long in town, Mr. Burkitt?"

"I had no intention of making any lengthened stay. Business, even in our small provincial way, *will* press, you know."

"How very unfortunate! I would do any thing to refresh Lord Royston's memory, I'm sure. A rising man, sir! And a fine match he's made, in every way, I'm told. The Cransdales are a wealthy family. A powerful political connexion too; at least it was in the late Earl's time. Young Earl in the Guards, I understand. Did you ever see Lady Constance Cranleigh—I beg her pardon—the new Lady Royston?"

"Oh dear, yes, often. An uncle of mine manages the estates, and was a great friend of the late Earl's. He has been almost a guardian to her and her brother. Indeed, I'm not sure that he was not regularly such under their father's will."

"Indeed! Is she so very lovely as they say?"

"She looked wonderfully well at the wedding, certainly."

"Oh, you were at it, were you? I'll tell you

what, Mr. Burkitt, my wife and daughters have a few young friends this evening after dinner. If I could bring such a live fashionable intelligencer down with me, I should appear a public benefactor. Drive down with me to Twickenham to dine and sleep. We'll find the pocket-book, and perhaps the notes that you're in search of."

It was as pleasant a way as any of passing his evening, so Keane accepted; and found it pleasanter than any when he also found Fanny Davenant in the Sherbrooke's drawing-room.

There was old friendship, it seemed, and even distant cousinhood between them and her family. She was there in fulfilment of an old standing engagement, to accompany them on a tour to the Lakes.

"Papa promised us this expedition last year," explained one of the Sherbrooke girls; "but it came to nothing. Then we were positively to have gone this year, in June. June went; July and August after them: and there's not much of September left now. But go at last we must and will, in spite of that tiresome business which always serves for an excuse."

"Tiresome business, indeed, Miss Nina! I should be fitter for drowning in lakes than touring round them if it wasn't for the tiresome business, I can tell you."

"Now, you naughty Pappy, you know you are as rich as a Jew, and can spare us a couple of months. Besides which, Walter has had his holiday, and will attend to the business as well as you could. What's more, if you don't take us, we mean to drown ourselves at the bottom of the lawn here, without going all the way to Westmoreland to find deep water. So beware!"

"Well, really, next week, after the Spanish bondholders have had their meeting, we'll try to make a start of it. I dare say, Nina, you'll keep us waiting for your bandboxes at last."

"How can you, Pappy, when I've been packed since Wednesday? I've half mind to have our boxes brought down into the hall this evening to convince you."

"And trip up your young lady friends as they come in, and tumble their new dresses? No fear of that, Nina. You'll stand in awe of them if not of me."

There was no long sitting over the wine of course that evening; but Mr. Sherbrooke had found the missing memoranda, and put Keane in the way to settle the matter in hand satisfactorily. He was much struck by the point of the quick and many questions which Keane put to him in this brief after-dinner conference.

"I wish you could have made my son Walter's acquaintance," he said. "You would have got on together. He has just your sharp way with him, and would have been delighted to put you up to what he calls the 'dodges' of the share market. He is a little too rash, though, Master Walter is; and if I didn't keep a tight rein on him, would run us into shaky places now and then."

There was a little music and a little dancing, and there were two or three charming seats in the conservatory, half hidden in flowery shrubs, for confidential conversation. Keane thought the evening had only passed away too quickly; and Fanny Davenant herself sighed to find it late so soon. Brother Walter, however, who had had his full month with the grouse, returned unexpectedly before the little party was broken up.

"I thought, sir, you might like me to be in the way for that Spanish meeting; and as the next steamer from the north would have been four and twenty hours late, I came away at once on hearing of it."

"Wise Walter! You couldn't have done better. I told you, Mr. Burkitt, he was a promising lad on

'Change. Allow me, though: Mr. Keane Burkitt, my son Walter. Odd enough; I was saying after dinner that I thought you would get on together, and as Mr. Burkitt was anxious for a little insight into some of the ways of stock-broking, that you were the man to give it him."

They did get on very well together after all the ladies had fluttered out of the conservatory, either home or up stairs to bed.

"Smoke's excellent for aphides," Walter observed, as he nestled down upon one of those delicious snuggeries among the flowers. "Wherefore even our woman folk tolerate my weeds here. Have one? They're Havannah direct, through one of that Spanish bondholding lot who are clients of ours."

"Couldn't put me in the way of getting a dozen boxes such?" quoth Keane, after a time, breaking an interval of balmy silence.

"Not over easy in the way of business, exactly; but I could introduce you to the man himself, who is rather a swell in a small way, and likes to be treated as such. If you've a talent for deferential tact, you might get some out of him as a favour. When do you leave town?"

Circumstances had altered since 11.30, A.M., on that same day, when he had spoken to Sherbrooke senior about the pressure even of provincial business. Hadn't he gathered that the Sherbrookes—and Fanny Davenant—would not be leaving for the Lakes till after that Spanish affair was over? Mr. Goring was equal to any call that Freshet was likely to make on the firm just then. Mr. Goring was rather fond of acting on his own responsibility. There were still some things to be done in town on Lord Royston's account. The tin boxes were safe at the Under-secretary's own house. His mother always liked to hear of his enjoying himself. Some insight into stock-broking was very useful to a man in his position. Such Havannahs were not obtainable from ordinary tobacconists. He had never seen Fanny look so well. He was pretty sure she was glad as well as astonished to see him; and in short:

"I had intended to run down home to-morrow or next day, but I've no sort of call to hurry. Shouldn't wonder if I were in town yet for a week or so."

"Look in on us in the City one day, then, and we'll pay our respects to Parkinson, Mendez and Co. It's Master Adolphus, 'Dolly Parkinson' they call him, that's my cigar man."

The next morning was lovely. Late as the season was, the summer, which had kept a sullen reserve in its own calendar months that year, seemed to bequeath to advancing autumn its warmth without oppressiveness, its radiance without glare. The film of moisture which the river had sent out at evening to hang over the flower beds and about the bushes, was not so thick but what its chilliness vanished, together with its apparent texture, in the earliest sunbeams after dawn. Keane was afoot betimes, and wandering down a shrubbery path already parqueted with golden lozenges of sunshine among the shadows of the leaves, came upon a little green sward at the bottom where there was a fantastic boat-house with pagoda roof. A slight rattling of chains was heard through its open door, and pleasant voices making fun of some disappointment.

Nina and Fanny Davenant had not expected that help was so nigh. They had fed the swans with sweet biscuit, until their sated statelinesses had paddled up-stream away. The bright ripple among the sedges tempted them to venture in pursuit; but the key was rusted in the padlock of the chain which held the boat, and they could not unfasten it. Keane could; and vaunted his own skill as steersman. So he took the rudder-strings, and each laughing girl an oar, and they rowed a losing stern-wager, as watermen say, after the swans.

"Isabelle is not up. I shouldn't wonder," cried Nina, looking at her watch, as they landed again by-and-by; "and I'm certain Walter isn't, after his long journey. It wants half-an-hour to breakfast yet."

There was talk at it, of course, about their boating adventure.

"I haven't seen the water so glassy pure for months," said Nina. "'Tis soft and warm as milk. I let my fingers dabble all the way back. It wanted no paddling to bring us down-stream."

"The day's intensely lovely," said sister Isabelle, who had certainly made her toilette in some haste after the half-hour bell had rung. "We've not had a regular boating party once this year. Why shouldn't we go to Hampton Court?"

"You'll blister your fingers if you're out of practice with your oars," quoth Walter.

"But we don't mean to row you lazy gentlemen," retorted Nina; "you may blister *your* hands, for of course *you* are to pull."

"Pull, indeed! We've something else to do than picknicking at Hampton Court. I'm going into the

City with the governor; so are you, are you not, Mr. Burkitt?"

"It's very cross of you, then, to spoil our pleasure. You know you never meant to be home for business this four or five days yet; so what can it signify? Don't you think they might stay with us now, Fanny?"

Keane held his breath, and busied himself with truant crumbs upon the tablecloth. Not daring to be all eye, he was all ear..

"It is a very lovely day," said Fanny Davenant, evasively.

"And you have never seen Hampton Court, have you?"

"Never!"

"But you should like to?"

"I think I should."

"Hear that!" cried Nina, "and crawl an inch towards the City if you dare."

"We'll send and ask the Perrys to come too. They've cousins with them who were here last night, Emily Bell and another; and they've a capital boat."

"Oh dear, then I'm in for it, I suppose," sighed Walter. "Emily Bell is nice-looking, isn't she?"

"You know she is," said Nina.

"Can we persuade you, Burkitt?" asked his new acquaintance.

"I want no persuasion," said he, venturing a look at last in one direction.

"What's all this about?" papa broke in, laying down his newspaper; "Nina promoting idleness as usual, and interfering with her brother's industry. You'll take a bed to-night here then again, Mr. Burkitt."

"I am ashamed of such intrusion, really—"

"Intrusion! my dear sir, how can you say so? Walter, see the trap brought round."

All clustered in the portico to see him off, but before the groom let the horses have their heads, a thought struck Walter.

"Oh, by the way, sir, if you should see that Gurkenheim to-day, Gurkenheim and Humpel; you know the man I mean; you had better say we'll have those hundred and odd Lahn-Mosel shares. They are the agents for the Frankfort house, I think."

The girls accompanied mamma back into the house. There was no interest for them in this. Keane stayed: he was much interested. The elder Sherbrooke pursed his mouth and shook his head.

"I don't half like it, Walter."

"Depend upon it, sir, it's all right about them.

I only wish I could afford the risk entirely upon my own account. They'll be at thirty per cent. premium before Christmas: mark my words."

Still Paterfamilias shook his head. His dutiful son chafed at his incredulity.

"He won't dispose of them in two lots, or I would ask you to take half of them for me myself, I would."

Thirty per cent. by Christmas! Keane couldn't resist it. In his excitement he grew suddenly familiar.

"I say, Walter, my boy, let me go shares with you."

"You're a trump!" said Walter. "You make the best bargain with Gurkenheim you can, sir, and buy the lot for us. All right, Tim!"

Tim gave the nags their heads. Neat steppers they were. Paterfamilias was many hundred yards upon his way to the great money market before Keane's foot was back on fairy ground again. Fairy ground! The ground on which the sunbeams of soft eyes are falling. Good ground, so those soft eyes be pure, to be trodden, once a life, even by the feet of young stockbrokers or young country solicitors. All day long the charmed light was beaming where Fanny went and Keane went with her. It was an enchanted river up which the twinkling oars propelled a magic boat. Those saucy swans, whom they did overtake at last, might have had rings and chains of fairy gold about the down of their white curving necks for all that he knew to the contrary. The trim walks and pleached alleys of the royal garden were kept, undoubtedly, by fairy gardeners; fairy cooks alone could have given such flavour of ambrosia to cold chicken and lobster salad; fairy butlers only such sparkle of nectar to the solitary tumbler of pink champagne.

Yet, after all, it was a social party. Grouped together almost the live-long day. There was but little of that separation by twos, not uncommon on occasions such as these. Not three significant sentences passed between her and him.

A pair of gloves of hers, however, lay on the seat near to the rowlock of Keane's oar, as they were dropping down-stream with the tide again that evening. It seemed an awkward rowlock, somehow, and out of order; for Keane slipped his oar once or twice. Perhaps it was in fixing it, that he contrived so quietly to launch one of the little gloves overboard unperceived. She had forgotten them altogether in stepping out of the boat on the little green sward at the villa, when they reached home;

and turning back to look for them, as the others went up the shrubbery-walk, found Keane fastening that rusty padlock once again.

Oh! was that her glove? Then the other, which he had seen swirling in a little eddy by the willow-bank on the eyot, must have been its fellow. He had seen it, but did not like to interrupt that glee just then.

Well, never mind; let her have the other.

"The other, indeed! Of what possible use could that be to you now?"

"There is no knowing. I may have a corresponding odd one somewhere. I always wear that colour, and the same shade of it."

"Indeed! Well, let me carry it at least up to the house, Miss Davenant."

He did, and, after all, forgot to return it there. She, too, forgot to claim it, although they met again, two days after, by a singular coincidence, at the last horticultural fête for the season, in the grounds at Chiswick; although Keane dined, another evening, down at Twickenham; although he was there with Walter Sherbrooke—they seemed to get on famously together—to see the party start at last *en route* for the English lakes. What could Keane Burkitt have meant by whispering to her at breakfast, that morning of the start—

"We shall be counting the days at Freshet, Miss Davenant, till that wearisome tour is over?"

CHAPTER VI.

There were more of them to count than they had reckoned on. The elder Sherbrooke found his holiday so pleasant, and heard from Walter that the money-market was so dull, that he prolonged it beyond the promised time. Then Nina caught a chill, and was so unwell, that on their second visit to Windermere, facing homewards, they had to wait a fortnight. Fanny Davenant was not quite well herself when they got back to Twickenham; and the city was so brisk again, that neither Mr. Sherbrooke nor his son could readily spare time to escort her home just yet. The journey to Freshet was too long to undertake alone; and the ladies'-maid had stayed at home with sister Sophy. Christmas came, and Fanny was still at Twickenham. Lord and Lady Royston were to spend it at Cransdale, and the earl himself would be at home on leave, after his first tedious campaign at the Tower. Mrs. Locksley once more accepted, not unwillingly, an invitation from her sister-in-law.

It was a sad disappointment to poor Mrs. Burkitt that her favourite Fanny should not be present at the little entertainments given and returned in honour of Lucy's presence. She felt so for her son, too, whose regret was visible, though he confided none of it to her yearning sympathies. He was anxious also about that venture in Lahn-Mosel scrip, which had not yet realised the bright hopes of Walter Sherbrooke, the prime minister for the Grand Duchy of Nassau being at odds with the Prussian Cabinet about the terms of concession to the Company. He had not burdened his mother's mind, however, with participation in this cause for apprehension, so that his wistfulness admitted, in her eyes, but of a single interpretation.

Miss Davenant of Lanercost observed it as well, and she, too, must needs interpret; for she was in Freshet, at her brother's, partaking with relish of its Christmas festivities. Her renewed acquaintance with "Lucy Burkitt that was," as she persisted in calling her, gave her considerable satisfaction. Reflection did but sanction and confirm the bequest of porcelain. She took the greatest interest, likewise, in Mrs. Locksley's intelligence from India; and having convinced herself, by close inspection of half-a-dozen Atlases, that Bombay lay comparatively near the Persian Gulf, entreated her to secure Ned's powerful and opportune co-operation in the procuring of a couple of pure-bred Persian cats.

"I dare say, dear, there's china to be picked up, rare and cheap, out there, as well; for I once knew the captain of an East Indiaman who put in at Calcutta regularly, on his way home from Canton."

"But my Ned's at Bombay, you know, Miss Davenant, which is out of the track of the China ships entirely."

"To be sure it is; but the mail steamers bring the China mails that way, so why not porcelain? Not that I want Mr. Edward Locksley to buy china for me there: young men don't understand that sort of thing, my dear; but they are very particular about their breeds of dogs, I know, which may teach them something about cats in that way. Besides, a cat is a sort of tiger; and I've always understood young Indian officers are very fond of tiger hunting."

Lucy laughed, as well she might, at such cogent

reasoning; nevertheless she wrote Ned word about the cats, having, indeed, herself, a lurking love of pussies. She stipulated for at least a kitten, should Miss Davenant secure, through Ned's exertions, the coveted pair.

The December "overland" had brought his answer, by return of post, to her announcement that Lady Constance was wedded indeed. She gathered from it that he had not swerved from his determination to accept, with resignation and with thankfulness, the definite closing of that one long chapter in his life; she was more certain of it when Lady Royston sent on to her a letter brought by the same Indian mail, containing these few lines:—

"Dear Lady Royston,

"God bless you, by the new name as by the old! I add, in honesty, the same prayer for him from whom you have the new. I thankfully accept the offer your last words made; and am, till death and after,

"Your true brother,

"NED.

"My love to Lady Cransdale and to Phil."

"Of course I had told Royston all, and showed

him this. He is profoundly touched by it, and says that if he dared, he would himself write back to Ned, and claim share in the brotherhood." So wrote the bride to Lucy.

The Christmas week was over. Miss Davenant was to return to Lanercost; but she had solved the enigma, for certain, at which she had been guessing, upon the countenance of her favourite, Keane Burkitt. He received a summons to wait upon her one evening at her brother's. Mr. and Mrs. Davenant and Sophy were gone to a party, whither she had refused to accompany them.

"Ah! my dear, doubtless I am depriving you of a pleasure. You would have been at the Thompsons' this evening, but for my fetching you here."

Keane said he should have been at home, or at his office, for he had two or three heavy bits of business on hand.

"No, no, my dear; don't tell me that. I am an old lady, yet I have kept a young heart."

Keane stared, but could not venture on any contradiction of the statement.

"The fact is, I have found you out."

"Found me out! In what, Miss Davenant?"

The little lady laughed like a parrakeet, and

shook her head from side to side with a ludicrous affectation of superior cunning.

"Found out the secret of your woebegone looks."

"Wonderful old woman!" thought he; "she must have got wind of that Lahn-Mosel business. Singular, too; but she has always dabbled in shares of some sort." All he said was: "I am sure, Miss Davenant, I had no notion my face told tales."

"It tells *me* tales; but I can offer consolation."

"Consolation, indeed!" He kept the thought to himself, however. There was little of that to get out of Gurkenheim and Humpel, hitherto.

"Now tell the truth. You know you are hit?"

"Hard, I fear," cried Keane, startled into candour. "How on earth came you to"—

"Never mind; I know it; but I doubt if she does."

"How should she?"

"How, indeed, unless you pluck up heart and tell her?"

"Tell whom?"

"My niece, to be sure."

"Tell her what?"

"Why, tell her that you have fairly lost"—

"My Lahn-Mosels?"

"Lahn-Mosels, sir! Is that what young men

call their affections now-a-days? What can the boy be thinking of? No, tell her that you have lost your heart to her."

With what countenance Keane fell from one wondertrap into another it were hard to say.

"Really, Miss Davenant, I could not presume"—

"Why not? Faint heart never won fair lady. I have made up my mind to the match; and if it takes place, I shall make a settlement on her at once. It will make my will plain sailing. First and last she shall have the two-thirds; her sister the other. There, that's all I have to say to you to-night. You know you ought to have been my son; at all events you shall be my nephew. Don't you like my niece?"

"Indeed, since you demand confession, I do with all my heart."

"Then why so bashful, such a smart young man as you are. Tell her so at once."

"At once!"

"Yes, what's the use of beating about the bush?"

"I'll write this evening, then."

"Write! fiddlesticks!"

"What else then? Shall I go"—

"Go! to be sure, go to the Thompsons' dance, and tell her what you have to tell."

"To the Thompsons' dance, Miss Davenant?"

"To be sure. Didn't you know Sophy was gone there with her father and mother to-night?"

One generous, impulsive outcry might have set all right, and saved them from the temptation which should follow. But his lips were locked. A meaner caution laid upon them the icy finger of that one sentence, "it will make my will plain sailing." As he balanced the probabilities of being able to persuade her to put one sister's name for the other, she proceeded to speak words which weighted the scale of wrong.

"It was only that primogeniture which ever made me hesitate. I always inclined to Sophy, and was glad to find that you did. She shall have the two-thirds as I said. Now, sir, be off to the Thompsons, and make yourself agreeable."

"The truth is, Miss Davenant, I am afraid of intruding. I don't know the Thompsons well; and on so delicate an errand one would wish"—

"Faint heart, I see; but the fair lady must be won. I have made my mind up to that, I tell you. Come here to-morrow morning, you shall have opportunity; I'll draw off mamma. So now, good night."

"Good night, Miss Davenant; but I can hardly say"—

"No need to! Keep your say for Sophy, sir, to-morrow morning."

Faint heart, indeed; but not faint with the faintness which modest self-distrust or generous exaggeration of another's worth makes amiable. Heart faint of purpose, because weakened by the merest and the meanest selfishness. Did he like Fanny so much more than Sophy as to make it worth his while to risk loss of the richer dower?

Such was, as near as possible, the shape in which his thoughts framed the definite issue for debate.

Fairyland is enchanting no less than enchanted ground. Why disenchant oneself? But fairy lore, as well as other, has its moral. He had always seen the sound sense of the warning against taking bribes of fairy gold. It turns to gorse blossoms or golden chain buds in the pockets of too trustful wights. With Fanny, and such sweets of Fanny's love, as fancy promised, he might get nothing else, What if Miss Davenant, offended, should cross her name out of the will altogether? Mere passion should be controlled by prudence; that is unquestionable moral, for fairy tale or tale "founded on fact."

Now, the old aunt's golden guineas were sterling coins, every one of them, not furze bush blossoms.

If a bird in hand be worth two in the bush, what should one say of two birds in the hand as against a solitary fairy warbler in the prickly bush of an eccentric old lady's prejudices?

Sophy's certain two-thirds against Fanny's possible none! Yet he did like Fanny, and there was her third possible, nay, probable still. Well, he would sleep on it.

And he slept, untroubled, whatever other conflict wrought within him, by one generous kindly thought of what effect his decision might have on Fanny Davenant's rest. When he woke, he woke to some kind of sorrow that he should have to choose between his softer and his sterner inclination. He could not even now decide on sacrificing what was dear to him, scarce thinking of what might be due to her.

The post brought him good news—news which, all things considered, might have brought influence to bear in Fanny's favour. There is always adventure in marriage; and a young man's heart, so readily venturesome, will be braced to further venture by success of any wager he has made against that chance which its thoughtlessness is too apt to worship as disposer of the coming years.

Keane's news was that the Prussian Cabinet had given way. The Nassau conditions were accepted. The Lahn-Mosel concession was complete. Gurkenheim and Humpel had themselves offered to repurchase from the younger Sherbrooke, at an enormous advance, the old unpromising scrip which they had sold him. It was actually quoted on the Frankfort exchange at thirty-two, and seven-eighths premium, and was rising still!

He was radiant at breakfast. All that his mother could elicit was that he had heard from the Sherbrookes; but joy stirred in her heart at hearing it. She knew but of one subject of correspondence with that family which might thus brighten the features of her son.

Presently Keane fell again into perplexity—not distressing, but such as leaves among the very wrinkles on the puckered forehead tokens that the doubts to solve are pleasing.

Thirty-two and seven-eighths! Should he realize or should he not? That was the question. Sherbrooke hadn't started it; but it called evidently for consideration. Thirty-two and seven-eighths, and rising still! Yes, rising still; and that at Frankfort! Could the Frankfort Rothschild be in it? Was their London house taking it up? Should that be so, there was no knowing what a figure it might touch. That offer to repurchase! Were Gurkenheim and Humpel operating on their own account, or were there bigger men behind!

"Oh dear! I wish I could run up to town."

He spoke, unconsciously, aloud, his mother heard him and rejoined—

"I wish you could, my dear; why shouldn't you?"

"Why shouldn't I what, mother?"

"Run up to town. I thought I heard you say you wished to. Do you want to pay the Sherbrookes a visit again?"

Keane smiled, amused at her true conjecture. His mood being such, she ventured for the first time—

"May I guess the attraction, Keane!"

But he was muttering, "Near upon thirty-three, by George!"

"Nonsense, Keane! She's hardly one-and-twenty."

"What, mother, who?"

"Why Fanny, to be sure, dear—Fanny Davenant."

"Nonsense!" he cried, half-startled by the word,

which recalled him from his calculations. He looked at his watch; the morning was creeping on towards noon. He felt that the little impatient aunt would be fretting at his non-arrival. What on earth should he do? He had not made up his mind, his thirty-two and seven-eighths had so excited him. But he must be moving; so, without further communication to his mother, he went out and made for Mr. Davenant's. There, he was shown up into the front drawing-room, where Little Miss Davenant was alone, holding up to the light and narrowly scrutinizing the quality of some tiny china cups brought from a curiosity shop for her approval.

"At last! What a laggard, to be sure! But I don't let grass grow under *my* feet, Master Keane. I have spoken to brother George, and he is well pleased it should be so. What's more, I've spoken to Sophy."

This was confounding. However, he made shift to say: "Did you, Miss Davenant? I am afraid your niece must have been surprised."

"Yes, she was, at first, a little. She said she had always thought you preferred her sister Fanny."

He had almost let the word escape his lips, which

should have done right and truth. But the greed of gold shifted suddenly the thought of his first success into the other scale again. Had not Miss Davenant said something of an immediate settlement upon Sophy? With such means in hand, in the present state of the share-market, what might not be done? He was silent. Miss Davenant chirruped on.

"I set that right, my dear, and told her how the truth stood. I said if ever you had showed her sister little attentions, it must have been for her sake. That you had kept your secret close; but that my little keen eyes had read it."

"May I venture to ask how Sophy Davenant received your intimation?"

"Here, ask for yourself;" and the brisk little woman opened a folding door into the inner drawing-room.

Sophy Davenant was there, looking puzzled, but very pretty. That circumstance itself was a fresh bait to such a nature as Keane's. "Well," he bethought him, "she was always the better-looking of the two."

"Here, Sophy," said her aunt, "here's Mr. Burkitt wants to make you understand that he never did like your sister Fanny half as well as you, you know. But that kind of explanation is given best in private."

She closed the folding door upon them, and went back to look for cracks in her china cups again.

When Keane Burkitt left the house, he had sacrificed Fanny Davenant and sold himself. Time was not given him to repent or draw back when the deed was done. Exulting in her own acumen, and in its easy securing of the happiness of her two favourites. Miss Davenant hurried matters on. Her brother and his wife, amazed to find how much she had it in her power to do for both their daughters, submitted with becoming meekness to her impatient dictation.

"I had rather thought it had been Fan, my dear," said Davenant one day to Mamma, intent upon the trousseau.

"Well, he was always very good friends with Sophy:" she answered, which indeed had so much truth in it as almost to justify her failure of perception in the time bygone. In fairness also to Sophy, Fanny herself allowed that she had kept a closer reserve than is sometimes kept between sisters. Neither now did her wounded and indignant heart give sign. A return of the indisposition she had already experienced in the autumn, pleaded her excuse for not coming home at once; and Sophy's protestations that she would not be married till dear Fan would be well enough to take her place among the bridesmaids, gave way before the peremptory temper of her aunt. That eager little orderer of nuptial rites had no farther reason to complain of apathy on Keane's part. Once the plunge taken, he swam with vigorous strokes. Legal delays were by his legal knowledge forced within their most restricted limits. What fortune Sophy was to receive from her own parents they, not unreasonably, tied up tightly for herself; but they could not with good grace, had they been so disposed, interfere in that sense with arrangements which depended upon the sole good pleasure of her aunt. Keane, by her kind confidence, would have his elbows free, and was impatient for the hour when he might strike out for the share market. His Lahn-Mosels were gone up to forty-five! But Sophy had no fairer ground of complaint against his attentiveness than her aunt against his expedition. If he had no depth of devotion to offer to any bride elect, of his own or another's election, he was wishful, for his own ease and pleasure then and thereafter, to win from her what devotion to himself he might. He did what he could to make her fond of him, and in so doing made himself, after a sort, fond of her. He had a knack of shelving unpleasant subjects of thoughts and feeling; and would have been comfortably rid altogether of any compunctions about Fanny, had it not been for his mother's looks. They wrought punctures, however, rather than compunction, fretting not grieving him. He came to think himself ill-used by her, and even then by Fanny. What right had they to dash with bitters his loving cup! Foolish fellow! This very dash gave "tonic" to the draught which got its sparkle from the bride's bright eyes.

It was a cheerful wedding, spite of dear Fan's absence; spite of the presence also of sorrow on his mother's face. Little Miss Davenant noted that, and even spoke of it to Keane.

"'Tis often the successful rival keeps the grudge the longest. Isabella won your father from me, but seems as if she couldn't quite forgive me now. I do believe she's vexed and out of sorts to see you marry a niece of mine, I do."

CHAPTER VII.

The first year of his marriage, and other speculations, was very prosperous for Keane. Sophy was, after all, the wife to suit him. In the mould of her character were none of those deep places which want more of the metal of strong affection to run into them to fill up what else would be dismal holes, than such husbands as he keep molten in their hearts' crucible. She shared his liking of small personal pleasures, and in surrounding herself with such, contrived to minister them in delightful abundance to him. She had withal sufficient spirit and sense of the importance of her own contributions to the elegance and luxury of the household not to spoil Keane in petting him as his mother had at last sunk into doing. She disciplined him into a gradual sense that pleasantness is easiest secured by being pleasant. Everyone allowed that Sophy Davenant had 'done wonders for that young man.' She thus put upon him a polish of popularity which was the only thing hitherto wanting to his position in Freshet. Magnified, of course by common report, her own wealth appeared to justify what otherwise might have been thought extravagant, the purchase and handsome fitting of a new house before the year was out. Not the most close-fisted or close-minded client of "Burkitt and Goring" intimated that the young couple were launching out imprudently. If anything, such as the costly knicknacks of young Mrs. Burkitt's new drawing-rooms seemed to denote a lavish disregard of expense, were not these things the doings of Miss Davenant of Lanercost? Two portly jars of almost priceless crockery sat swelling with continual affirmation of the exculpatory truth. Indeed it was very much to young Burkitt's credit that neither the smiles of such a pretty wife as Sophy, nor the cushioned chairs of such a luxurious home, could seduce him from assiduous attendance at his office. It got about, of course, likewise, that Lord Royston's affairs were in his hands entirely. And Lord Royston was "not one of your scatter-brain young nobles, sir, but a man of increasing weight and authority, sir; a man of whose confidence any firm of solicitors might be proud, sir; a man whose connexion might come to have political importance one day for young Burkitt, sir; whom we shouldn't be surprised to find nominated for Cawsley some of these fine mornings, sir. Snug little borough Cawsley, sir; spared by the Reform Bill; completely under Rookenham influence, my dear sir."

Keane's business, therefore, increased; more, indeed, than they knew that brought it to him. For the good folks of Freshet knew nothing of his increasing association with the business of his friends the Sherbrookes. With them, also, he stood, or rather kept on climbing higher and higher in the scale of esteem. He was not only successful, but deserved success, "for his happy audacity," said Walter; "for his wise caution," said Walter's father. The Sherbrooke girls had frowned at first a little on his marriage; for people have a way of floating on enchanted rivers, or treading on enchanted grounds which betrays them fairy-struck, to Ninas and Isabellas. Nevertheless, they, too, like good-natured girls as they were, came round to the charitable interpretation that Keane, after all, had only been paying due devoirs, by proxy, under the stately trees of Hampton and among the flowery tents of Chiswick. "Only remember, Nina, should any such nonsense take place with one of us, you know, it will be better, to prevent misunderstandings, that the queen regnant hold her own drawing-room, and courtesies be proffered to the sovereign alone in person."

Keane's countenance, the first time they saw him after the event itself, betrayed no embarrassment; so when, the next time, he brought up Sophy with him to Twickenham, and they saw the prosperous sunshine on her pretty face as well, they could no longer, in reason, think it treachery to Fanny, whom they loved rather the better, to shower congratulations and cousinly kindnesses upon her sister.

With his Aunt Lucy, Keane could lose nothing by reason of his conduct towards the elder of the Davenants. Mrs. Locksley was utterly ignorant of any such episode in his career. She was not unobservant, however, of the estrangement which circumstances seemed to be working gradually between his mother and himself. The working was subtle; but, perhaps, all the more unavoidable. Keane was, apparently, not in fault. He certainly had not said it in so many words; but he had given her to understand that it was entirely by her own choice that Mrs. Burkitt, senior, remained in the old house, when Mr. and young Mrs. Burkitt removed into the new. Though the younger lady's bearing towards the elder was unimpeachable, as all Freshet admitted, one could always understand that two mistresses make the easiest of households difficult. And, though age and widowhood had wonderfully softened her sister-in-law, Lucy could remember when there had been an imperious element in her character. Indeed, her brother himself—if her memory did not do injustice to Isabella—had hinted at an excess of that ingredient in it occasionally. Doubtless, all things considered, it was as well that mother and daughter-in-law should be spared all possibility of domestic collision. Yet, little by little, the conviction grew that Keane in his new house, not twice five hundred yards from his old home on the Marine-parade, lived farther from his mother than did her own dear Ned from her across those thousand weary leagues of land and sea. She was ashamed to think how often her mind would turn to such a thought, and speculate upon the truth or falsehood of it, and upon the causes of the fact, if fact it were. There may be sometimes lurking malice of a very venomous kind in studying the comparative anatomy of our blessings and those of others. An exultation borne of envy rather than of true thankfulness creeps over us.

Yet there was a consolation which seemed to distil kindly from the contrast, with no need of any fire of envy, hatred, malice, or uncharitableness, to quicken its production. However it might be between her nephew and his mother, she need not hide from her own eyes what might have been between herself and her own son.

Supposing Lady Constance had returned his love. Supposing she had been a few years younger, or he a few years older than the case had been. Supposing that no difference of rank or wealth had parted them.

What then? They would have gone out, hand-in-hand, into a world which was not hers. Or else, absorbed in love for one another, they might have rounded out a life for their ownselves, which might, like other round things, have touched hers at some one point alone.

Whereas, whatever tenderness was in her son's heart, it nestled down in her. The manner of his ripening into manhood now was such as made him, after truer child-like sort than ever, still her child.

Who goes from home may keep it heart's home more heartily than even he who stays.

Lady Cransdale also came to sense of this. In her delicate nobleness she determined to let Lucy read her thought and feeling if she would. Not thrusting her own heart's book agape under the soul's eyes of her friend, as a less graceful generosity might do; but letting the leaves flutter open in the soft breath of motherly talk.

Phil was doing well in the Guards. Very popular, very gay; not so very reckless of expense, though just a little extravagant. She heard from the Colonel of his battalion,—for he himself didn't tell her much of his military matters,—that there were many youngsters of his standing as ready as he to shirk tedious duties; not that he was considered a model young officer by martinet adjutants. She couldn't make out that he read anything except a few sporting novels, though he drew a good deal and had some talent, rather a dangerous one, for caricature. She had heard something of a flirtation with a Lady Maude Cassilis; but not from Phil himself, who was discreet, if desultory, in such little affairs. Not that she thought there was anything serious in it. The Cassilis people were not of her own intimates. Constance, who met them oftener, was not much taken with her.

"Prickly plants of disappointment spring up in so many shapes! Yet some have flowers of sweet afterscent. So sweet, one is content to lay them in one's bosom, thorns and all."

Lucy caught her meaning and was not ungrateful.

"Tell me something about Lady Constance, I can't quite frame to call her Lady Royston yet."

For Lucy knew that the mother's heart had not a word to speak on that score, but such as welled up in overflow of perfect trust and love.

"Dear Con is well and happy. Do you know I sometimes feel," said Lady Cransdale, with an effort, "as if I had to crave your pardon Lucy, still, for the delight that marriage gives me; but, indeed—"

"Indeed, dear Lady Cransdale, it reproaches me deservedly to hear you say so. It was to make and snatch an opportunity that I brought in your dear daughter's name?"

"An opportunity for what?"

"Redeeming a promise which there should have been no need to make: which made, should have been long since redeemed."

"Riddles, my dear, dark riddles!"

"You shall read them. Do you remember that bright sunshiny day, now nearly two years gone, when you came in there, at that very window, bringing in for me the prickly bough? You understand me?"

She nodded.

"The thorns pricked as I took it. At the smart I turned upon you; rebelling, indeed, against another than this dear hand."

She took her old friend's into hers, as they sat on the same sofa there, and raised it to her lips.

"I was unjust, abrupt, and rude; but, before you went, I made a promise to beg your pardon some time more explicitly. And I have failed to do so, till to-day. Will you forgive me?"

"Hardly; for having spoken thus." Clasping the hand which held hers.

"Well, then, I demand a pledge. Ill-disciplined hearts like mine are often unbelievers."

"Whatever pledge you please, dear Lucy."

"This, then; that henceforward you speak as freely to me of your daughter as your son. I have noticed a constraint—which showed your kindness—but also my little deserving it."

For her rebellion against that other gracious Hand, Lucy, long since, had humbled her own soul in secret. After this open confession, she seemed to be returned in truth into her own true self. She was again meek-hearted Lucy, perhaps more truly than before. She thus regained the blessing of the meek-spirited, of whom it is written, that "they shall possess the earth." It was a re-possession of it once more to think, to speak, to feel, to act, heart to heart with her old friend again. The space between the Lodge and Cransdale House shrunk back into some hundred yards of daisy dight green lawn. The sandy waste which had been intervening disappeared, and, happily, before the bones of loving memories lay bleaching on it.

Towards the end of that same year Robert Locksley had a sharp fit of illness, not such as put his life in any danger; but such as, happening just when it did, might have wrought much confusion in the accounts of the estate and some delay in necessary business. His nephew was at hand, however, and could be trusted, as no stranger could, to act by his directions and in his stead. Ned, out in India, felt something like self-reproach when news reached him that his father needed help of such sort; but he consoled himself by thinking, how much more fit his cousin must be to supply it—by virtue of his calling—than he could have been hi m-self even had he been following a university career. He wrote to Keane a letter of hearty thankfulness, expressing a hope that not only he but his bride, would play son and daughter's part by the dear ones whom he had left, as it were, childless.

Lucy, notwithstanding, could not and did not, invest Keane's wife with the same favourable prejudice as himself. Though she knew nothing of her sister-in-law's disappointment, she shared it after a fashion. Fanny Davenant was much more to her mind than Sophy. In virtue of the new connexion between their families she cultivated more intimate acquaintance with her, persuading her, nothing loath, to spend some months at Cransdale.

Strange power even of unconscious sympathy stored in true gracious hearts! The Countess took to Fanny, as her friend Lucy, did. From these two women, over whose daily lives the thorny sprigs laid in their bosoms shed such sweet perfume, she seemed to learn insensibly the secret of disembittered resignation. For resignation, also, has varieties. The quality of Fanny Davenant's might have been imperilled, at the first, even by one who felt for her so heartily as did Keane's mother. Benevolence is sometimes selfish, no less than indifference. Compassion may overflow to ease the compassionate rather than the sufferer. Wounds will not always bear the balm of pity. Its first drops, especially, require the spare dropping of a sensitive hand. There is an inflammation of resentful pride soon heated by their smart. Mrs. Burkitt's schooling in the craft of charity was not yet deep enough to make her know this well. Else she would not have said, one day, after Keane and his wife had but just left her drawing-room:

"I thought it had been you, dear Fanny, not your sister. I still think it should have been. I am so sorry for you."

Happily these words were spoken after, not before, that soothing time at Cransdale. The flush, indeed, could not but glow upon the poor girl's cheek, the tears but tremble on her eyelashes. Yet she found the rare grace, even whilst wincing at the pain, to pardon the ignorant cruelty of her would-be comforter. That rare grace gifted her likewise with a singular spirit of discernment. She divined what manner of hope had drawn the widow's heart towards herself. She divined how the travail of that heart had been in vain. Keane's wife was to it as a still-born daughter. Divining this, she learnt to pity her own pitier, and bent her mind with subtle delicacy, to minister some consolation. Noble task ever: and sweet task at the last! Yet often difficult, often tedious, sometimes repugnant, sometimes almost desperate. Bodily life is precious, and ministering to it often costly. Spiritual life is priceless, and ministering by so much costlier. Whoso shall reckon acts of spiritual mercy cheaper to be done than bodily, shall most times grievously misreckon the true cost of either.

Robert Lockaley was hale and active again before the passing months brought the birthday of an heir to Rookenham. It was an event for the whole countryside, and the christening was a grand affair. Keane and Sophy, herself not long after to become a mother, received and accepted an invitation to the festivities. Fanny, though pressed by Mrs. Lockaley to come on the great occasion to Cransdale, refused, and spent the time chiefly in company with Keane's lonely mother. It was just then that, to her surprise she received and, without hesitation, refused, a very different invitation. Far greater would that surprise have been, had she known that Walter Sherbrooke's offer had been instigated by Keane himself. For Miss Davenant, of Lanercost, had long since duly executed her last will and testament: and Keane's hint to his friend, that his sister-in-law, "a charming girl, as I need not tell you, my good fellow," was down in it for so many thousands, was not thrown away upon the speculative young stock-broker. Who knows but what Keane Burkitt thought he was making honourable reparation? Unless, indeed, he simply wished to have it under her own hand in the parish register, that her score against him was even in court of conscience cancelled. Men have the queerest notions of a satisfactory schedule for exhibition to that inward court. The satisfaction, such as it might have been, was denied.

Amidst these vicissitudes, the most even tenor of life beyond a doubt, was his who for adventure and enterprise had become an exile. Ned's letters were uniform, and to any but a mother almost monotonous. In all those months one only incident, by no means an exciting one, had marked them. He had repaid, by draft upon his regimental agent, the five hundred pounds his father had sent him after his gambling freak at Chatterham. But a change was nigh at hand, and a life-stage opening out before him, so long and so full of varied event that even a more formal life-story than this might be compelled to furnish only such indications of its character as fragments of the man's own correspondence may reveal. If even these be tedious, skip but one chapter, impatient reader, they shall fill no more.

CHAPTER VIII.

Peernaghur, &c., &c.

Dearest Mother,

You may well ask what hurried me here and launched me thus upon a new and unexpected course. To tell you the truth, it was the resolute kindness of Miss Florence Barrington. Some days before his Excellency made me a formal offer of this appointment I had a conversation with her which equally surprised and moved me. She had read my mind as in an open book. She had understood that the very passport to her uncle's good will, Lord Royston's recommendation, was to me a barrier against its cordial acceptance. She had even penetrated into the secret of the strangely mingled attraction and repulsion, which her own likeness to Lady Constance exercised upon me from the first moment of introduction. It was in the name of Lady Constance that she begged me not to refuse another offer of her uncle's should he make one. You would have been as much struck, I believe, as I was, with her tone and manner in making an apology for mentioning the name which I have been learning to divest of some among the feelings which have clung to it. She said, that "worthy love working in worthy natures, might fulfil other ends than what it had thought its own." She said, that "judging Lady Constance by herself, she was certain that she would need some consolation for having won what she could not accept and so repay; and that there could be no such consolation as to know that some such worthy end had been fulfilled in me." As she spoke, the voice was not Constance's; but the spirit which thrilled in it was hers, indeed. I will be open with you, mother dear; it flashed across me that it were no treason, scarce a transfer, to surrender to such a counterpart of her own self what it were insult now to call hers. I almost wished I could feel for Florence Barrington what I have felt for Constance Cranleigh, and could dare to say so. Something killed the thought as it arose; partly the likeness to Constance, partly something else, which seemed to frown against it, as if but one degree removed from the wrong of indulging the old affection.

There now, that is my last bit of sentiment, as far as I know, for ever and a day. Forgive it, as I pass on. What she next said was this, that she and her cousin Rosa, hearing that her uncle's government intended to create this post had entreated him to nominate myself. Was ever any thing so kind, yet ever any thing so audacious? The governor, of course, said I was too young in years and service, objections which they met by the most undeserved commendations of my character and abilities. Only fancy his Excellency beset by such advisers? Well, he offered the appointment to a Mr. Plowden, a civilian of superior attainments and some length of service. He had just obtained long leave home, and could not forego the hard-earned and dear privilege. Then a Captain M., whose name I suppress for reasons, would have been nominated; but something in his regimental accounts would not come out satisfactorily. Delay could not be brooked; so the Governor, I presume in despair—he said, in his official note, on account of my readiness in acquiring native languages—adopted the suggestion of his nieces. I had short warning; bought three horses and a few baggage ponies out of the money which that too generous pappy returned after all my trouble in saving it; and here I am on the north-west bank of the Nerbuddah. That is what brought me here. Where it has brought me, and wherefore, I will expound in some future epistle. There's a row begun about a herd of buffaloes which has been driven from one of my villages; we are considerable cattle-stealers hereabouts you must know; and the righting of such wrongs won't allow dawdling. So good-bye, dear mother, love and duty to my father, kind remembrances to all Cransdale folk.

Your ever loving and dutiful.

Ned.

Peernaghur.

My very dear Father,

I should think it stranger still if you *could* exactly strike off my whereabout upon the map. I have heard that they have at Indore an old chart of the province on copper, supposed to have been etched by a Chinese engineer for a Mogul emperor; but it is of doubtful authenticity, and, little as I know of surveying, I believe myself to be the most scientific surveyor the country has seen since the problematical Chinaman. As for the history of the district it is the old one in India. A princely family suffers from plethora of moral vice and dwindles into physical atrophy. Then come adoptions and substitutions of one kind and another. Even such attempts to perpetuate legitimate authority are frustrated by endless intrigues and stained by repeated assassinations. Unwomanly women, and creatures of crime, whom one can't call men, tyrannize in the name of this or that infant of spurious origin. Whether in league or at feud, their unvarying system of government is that of misrule, rapine, and cruelty. A rabble soldiery, Arabs, Pathans, Mekranees, Poorbeahs, and what not, overawe the capital; but elsewhere the central government is powerless, except for occasional raids. Every landowner turns his house into a citadel, and runs a rampart of baked mud, loopholed for musketry, round his principal paternal village. Therein he resists the agents of such central authority as may assert itself foı a time; and thence he sallies out to plunder weak outliers. This kind of anarchy seethes and scorches for years within the borders, and then overflows, to set on fire pleasanter pasturages outside, owning British rule. Annexation not seeming immediately desirable, that sort of compromise is made, which consists in sending a British Resident to tyrannize beneficently over maleficent tyrants. His duties become at once intricate and overwhelming. Distant dependencies haven't a chance of his care; so the Bombay people send him one Ned Locksley to do the work as assistant on the frontier. Of course I am theoretically the subaltern and slave of Sir Joseph Buckle; but as the distance between us is great and the road a track; as our last mail-bag bearer, but two, was eaten by an alligator, and the last shot with poisoned arrows by the Bheels, I don't receive many orders, and act upon still fewer, being practically independant. Talking of Bheels, I may proceed to say, that though my district is peopled by various races, intermingled in habitation though distinct in blood, that race is in numerical majority. An outcast and down-trodden race, whose unrecorded history stretches back into remotest ages, before the fairer-skinned stronger-limbed herdsmen from the Himalaya streamed in conquest over Hindostan, before the wild riders of the central Asiatic steppes piled cavalry saddles into Mongol thrones. Poor fellows! Even their Rajpoot tyrants seem to make a grotesque acknowledgment of their original title to the soil. Every new made Rajah submitted, and, for aught I know, submits to have his forehead smeared with blood drawn from a Bheel's finger and toe, when he assumes the turban of sovereignty. Spite of which, the fiscal officers of these same Rajahs have been allowed to take a Bheel's life at convenience without trial, form, or ceremony. Little wonder if the bolder or more despairing of them, crouching in the jungle or burrowing in caves and clefts, turn thieves, marauders, shedders of man's blood, showing none of that mercy which they never receive! A Bombay missionary told me that he was among them once, and actually received this answer to his invitations:

"Even men drive us from their homes, how should God let us come near?"

Their faces have literally "gathered blackness," and in hue, if not in feature, might justify the term I so dislike of niggers. All are not, however, jungle tribes or hill tribes. Some live in alluvial plains, house in frail villages, practise an imperfect system of irrigation, and till with the rudest of instruments the richest of soils. Oh, dear me! I am writing like a guide-book—for a limited class of tourists, I fear. Couldn't you send Cousin Keane out to me, since you can't come yourself.

You say, which I don't believe, that he manages things at Rookenham as well as you can at Cransdale. At all events, then, he could help me with work of which the bare thought confounds. It's not that aforesaid irrigation: only think if you could come to me, the planner of the Cransmere watermeads! It's not so much the agricultural improvement: only think again, I say, if you could come, the President of the St. Ivo's Farming Association! It's the assessment and land-tax work appals me. We call it making a settlement, and a pretty settling I am like to make of it! Sir Joseph is right enough, though. We must both fix and collect the revenue, were it only to cut off all the oppressions upon that score of the ruffianly clique which keep the nominal sovereignty. But at Eton, in my time, none of us knew the multiplication table; and even at home I never came right out at the other end of "Long Measure." Imagine, therefore, what I am likely to do with coins, and weights, and measures, outlandish, and as old as Alexander, may be Noah.

As by-play, I am creating a police, entirely of cow-stealers, armed with bows and arrows. The inspectors alone, tell Hutchins, have trowsers, and take them off when ordered on duty. How strangely things fit in a man's life! My crossbow practice, with dear old Phil, under the cedars, tells here, and has conciliated vast respect among the "cowguards black." They had an archery meeting, after a sort, and shot for a pot of ghee, which, to their intense astonishment, I won. But bows and arrows won't serve my turn, nor even matchlock men, nimble and swift marchers, as my barefoot brigade can show themselves. As sure as fate, I must raise a squadron of irregular horse; or the dacoits, professional robbers, to say nothing of contumacious and refractory landowners, with well mounted tenants wielding sharp swords, will be too bold and quick for me. But for this I must have superior authorization. Send me out a two-ounce rifle, with all necessary fittings. Consign to Briggs and Chundurree, Bombay. The tigers have eaten two of my village Bheel wood-cutters of late; and though I mean to have a shot at them with the rifle I have by me, I want something heavier and more reliable. Expense no object—so the weapon be first-rate. If you know any rough and ready treatise upon road-making, or any book—say, for instance, published in some enterprising colony—which gives receipts for such a manufacture, send it, please; also any book on Egypt or Holland, or both, treating of dikes, embankments, and the like. I have little enough time for reading, as you may guess, just now. But your little Greek Testament never leaves my person, nor does a day pass without a dip into it. I have no notion what may be stirring even in the Indian world, much less the European, our dawks having exceeded of late their usual exemplary irregularity, and left me newspaperless. Remember me to Cransdale in general. Kiss dearest mother for her and your ever dutiful and loving.

NED.

Mhawulpore.

Dearest of Mothers,

You say you are glad I read the New Testament. I have need, too, were it only to qualify my practice of the Old. You may wonder what I mean by that; but the fact is, that besides the identity of many Oriental customs, manners, and modes of thought and speech, the whole tenor of my life, and of those around me, the primitive character of their virtues, and, unhappily, still more of their vices and crimes, together with the kind of attempts I make to encourage the one and check or root out the other, all combine to make me feel as if I were gone back in the flesh as well as in the spirit to the days when there were "Judges in Israel." Last time I was in our hill country I lived for coolness in a cave, and couldn't help thinking of David in Adullam. The description of his sojourn there, in the First Book of Samuel, will give an account of my mode of life, word for word.

"Every one that was in distress, and every one that was in debt, and every one that was discontented, gathered themselves unto him; and he became a captain over them; and there were with him about four hundred men."

I don't know whether David had opportunity to punish their misdeeds, as well as in some measure to redress their grievances. I try to do what little I can in both ways. I wish I could do what David tried to do for them, if, indeed, I read somewhere, it was to that nondescript gathering that he cried, "Come ye children and hearken unto me: I will teach you the fear of the Lord." I cannot, however, well play the missionary among them, though I endeavour to act, and make them see that I do, upon the same principles as a true missionary would preach. I have written, by the way, to Mr. Mavor, a Company's chaplain at Bombay, much interested in such matters, to see what can be done in a formal and regular manner if possible, upon this head.

My mission, however, is clear enough, to preach by deed rather than word, with an occasionally sharp-edged commentary, the astounding doctrines, as they are reckoned hereabouts, that right may possibly consort with might, a strong ruler be just, and even a just be merciful. Grand preaching that, mother dear, the preaching of a law not other than an introduction to the Gospel—is it not? Pray for your boy, dear, that he may have a wise head, true heart, and—I fear you must add—strong arm, to deliver his sermon.

To-day, however, I am in the Book of Judges, as I said, sitting literally, like Deborah, under a palm tree. Under a clump of them, indeed, a "tope," as we say, clustering trees, under whose shadow my tent is spread. My tent-pitchers, I must tell you, had almost a pitched battle for the site with the monkeys. Had they been Hindoos, reverence might have driven them, the tent-pitchers, into the open, when the sacred grinners showed fight. I should have been prettily grilled. But my poor Bheels will pelt a monkey without compunction, though they will offer a fowl in sacrifice to the demon of tigers; so the apes are expelled, and I am in possession of the tope. It is not often that my cutcherry business offers any thing as interesting as the case I have been at all day. I don't often stuff my writing with Indianisms, but have probably expounded cutcherry work to mean the labour of the magistrate's desk before now. It was a case of cattle-stealing, complicated by manslaughter, or murder; it is hard to classify the deed impartially. Nothing unusual, you will say, if you have not forgotten my former letters. Case and complication alike commonplace. True for you, Madam; but the curious, unusual, and interesting circumstance was this, that the counsel for the defendant was a woman—his wife; and most acutely did she plead his cause. I should premise that the Bheel women enjoy considerable social liberty, though sharing, as do the women of all savages, a cruel disproportion of household and field labour. They have, however, much influence over their husbands, and not undeservedly. The man upon his trial was one Bikhu, a Bheel from Malwa. The evidence against him pretty clear. My puggees, or trackers, whose skill, or instinct shall I call it, even among these wild tribes, is wonderful, pronounced his name without a moment's hesitation, when the footmarks of the marauder were first come upon. Through jungle and over sandy rock they had followed him with the unerring sagacity of blood-hounds; and, assisted by a detachment of my "cowguards black," had effected his capture, much to the astonishment and rejoicing of the country side. Taxed with the robbery, he admitted it without blushing. I beg leave to say that I have seen the accusing flush even under these dark skins. Like a true Bheel, he was a fatalist, and threw the blame of his malpractices upon the powers above.

"Sahib," said he, "I am Mahadeva's thief. But great is your good fortune. Let me go. I will not rob during your raj, or reign."

I was half inclined to take him at his word: thought indeed of offering to so frank a character an inspectorship in the cowguard. But it appeared, further, that in the scuffle a villager had been killed, and the arrow which stuck in him was found to correspond in length, shape, feathering, and I can't say what other conclusive particulars, with those of Bikhu's quiver. Now cow-stealing, though meritorious, if successful, is admitted on this border to be punishable if detected. Manslaughter is a minor consideration, so far as public justice is concerned.

The punjayets, a sort of jury of five, presided by their patils or headmen—whom I am scrupulous in associating with me whenever circumstances will allow—don't trouble themselves about avenging bloodshed as a social offence, but leave it, as of old in Israel, to the avenger of blood and private retribution. The slain cow-herd having no relatives, and the chances being against any one's retaliating in juggra or blood-feud-fray, Bikhu thought himself safe, and was painfully candid; went even so far as to express a hope that the arrow would be returned to him, being of superior make and workmanship. This was awkward for me, who, though no patron of cow-stealers, endeavoured without offending popular prejudice, to magnify, as against theirs, the crime of manslayers. I shook my head and muttered of rope. Bikhu seemed, on the whole, resigned. Then uprose and outspake a woman; a girl, we should have called her in England. I inquired her age; she was just fourteen, with as beautiful and interesting a countenance as I have seen in India.

"I am Thakali," she said "the wife of Bikhu. Hear me, Sahib, and do the thing which is just."

"Sahib, those are *your* soldiers," pointing to a brace of sentries with drawn swords outside the tent; "bid them slay Thakali. *You* will have killed her, not they. Bikhu is the slave and soldier of

Badaga. When he said 'shoot,' Bikhu shot; but Badaga slew the cow-herd. Do justice, Sahib."

Knowing what I now know of Bheels, I felt that if her facts were correct, her argument was unanswerable. Badaga was a gentleman whose name had reached my ears before, a petty marauding chieftain, whose influence in his own region and over his kindred families was paramount. Clansmen are cousins here, as among the Celtic Highlanders. Change but the name and Scott wrote of my Bheels—

"Each trained to arms since life began,
Owning no tie but to his clan,
No oath, but by his chieftain's hand,
No law but—*Badaga's*—command."

It seemed certain, upon investigation, that the chief himself had been present at this particular foray; and, so far, Thakali's assertion, that her husband had acted under orders, was borne out. I remembered to have seen it laid down by no less an authority than Sir John Malcolm, that in such phases of Indian barbarism as I must meddle with, it is wisest, safest, and most effective, to punish the chief for the crime of his subordinate. Thakali's plea chimed in with that great oriental statesman's policy.

Wherefore after solemn admonition, Bikhu was reprieved. Even to a fatalist life is sweet. He was certainly pleased; but the poor girl was beside herself with gratitude and joy.

I have sent a message to the chief to say that if he does not come in, make his salaam, and bring back the cows, or pay for them within four days of its receipt, he must reckon with me, and so forth.

Such being the case, Bikhu and Thakali both declare they dare not revisit him, and that they must starve, unless I take compassion on them. I have told them they may eat my rice till I can otherwise provide; and therewith ended this day's cutcherry.

Whether my gallows bird will make a confidential servant, time will show. I hear he is very fond of horses, having stolen a good many, as most Bheels do: not much of a rider, but having a knack of grooming vicious ones. I dare say my Syces would be delighted to turn Abool Harg, my chestnut Arab, over to him. . . . .

Peernaghur.

Dearest Father,

Tommy Wilmot has just killed our man-eater. That is the great news of the day, so I hasten to record it. There's a shouting and yelling and beating of drums and gongs in the village at this moment, which, if it wasn't for the jungle, you could almost hear in Cransdale; but bamboo deadens echoes, where it grows thick.

To begin at the beginning, you may remember that you sent out last year a two-ounce rifle: a first-rater it was and is. But really business grew so fast upon me that live tiger and torn villager were getting to be both drugs in the market. I had killed some five or six brutes my first year, partly for sport, partly for policy, not to say religious enthusiasm.

I see you lift your eyebrows. But the fact is, that Waghia, as they call him, "the lord of the tigers," was the most popular divinity in these parts when I first came; and I couldn't bear to see my poor Bheels bow down to clay caricatures of this bloody monster. There was one rude stone image, at a shrine on the jungle's edge, some three miles distant, which was always richly bedaubed with votive oil and vermilion, and on whose head endless cocoa nuts were broken for offerings. I hated and longed to smash it; but was afraid at first of kindling some fanatical outburst. One evening, however, I became aware that Bheel votaries of Waghia cherish some of that latent contempt for him which makes Neapolitans flog St. Januarius. For riding slowly near the shrine, a little before sunset, I overheard two villagers, Gopaji and Devaji by name, reviling their idol in round terms. "You fellow!" cried Gopaji, "I gave you pulse and broth, and a chicken; yet you killed my buffalo!" "Broth and a chicken!" screamed Devaji; "I gave you three chickens and a goat, yet you carried off my child! What more do you want, you rascal?"

This was a great opening. "My good friends," said I, riding up, "men can kill tigers as well as tigers men. It's a disgrace for a man to worship a savage brute. And what's the good of it? He will fill his belly, sacrifice or no." Up jumped Gopaji and Devaji from their knees, on which they had been making this recriminatory poojah, *anglicè* worship. They scratched their thinly bearded chins as they gaped on me; but with no polemical anger as it seemed.

"Very fine talk for Sahibs," at length said Gopaji, with that stolid cunning wherewith the world over the true "clod" tries to trip his adversary; "Sahib rides a horse as wicked as Waghia, and almost as great a jumper: poor Bheels walk afoot. Sahib carries sword and gun, such poor Bheels as we, carry clubs, and haven't even bows and arrows."

The inference was obvious: if I were in their plight, I should compromise, he meant, with pulse and broth and chickens. You know my readiness to kindle at any spark of defiance.

"I am not afraid of Waghia, my good friend, Gopaji," I said, in answer: "the same only God who made him made me, and made me his master. I have little time for skikar, as you know; but I'll hunt till I kill four tigers in that jungle here, on one condition."

"The Sahib is Lord of all, and may make any that pleases him."

"Well, if I kill four tigers, in this neighbourhood, you shall own that Waghia is beaten: and I may have leave to smash this stone."

I kicked it slightly, with contempt, as I put the question.

"Smash him at once, Sahib," cried the time-serving Gopaji.. Devaji himself took heart, and spat therewith upon the image of the brute that had eaten his child.

"Not till I have fought him four times on foot alive, and brought him in four times dead."

Wherefore, I went a tiger-hunting with Bikhu,

who is a puggee, a shikaree, and an esprit-fort, as it turns out, into the bargain. He was an admirable assistant, tracks like a sleuth-hound, and stands as stiff as a well-broken pointer to game. I killed my first four in two months' time, and smashed Waghia with pomp—*coram populo.* I feasted three villages on this occasion; and as I gave a rupee to every Bhât, or wandering priest of the Bheels for ten miles round, no theological objections were started. But I was a good deal away from here for some months after, round by Torân-Mall and the Mhawulpore Hills, a spur of the Vindhya on your maps. Waghia looked up again, and wood-cutters down. Two of them were killed—one of them a cousin of Gopaji's. My *prestige* was shaken. A Bhât of some popularity, who was away on a pilgrimage when the rupee went round, and got none, began to mutter the Bheel for "Nemesis." I like the shooting well enough, but had no time on hand, being heart and soul in my drill for the Irregulars, who recruit very fast, I am happy to say. Bikhu is bold, but can't manage the two-ounce. The crisis was pressing. I luckily bethought me of Tommy Wilmot, sergeant by this time, and applied for him to the colonel. It was a dear delight to see a Cransdale face and hear a Cransdale tongue, as you may fancy, in the Trans-Nerbuddah. But better still, I had rightly conjectured Tommy's true vocation. He took to the two-ounce as if he were its father, and to the jungle as if it were his cradle. My fame as shikaree is gone—utterly eclipsed by Tommy's, who slays tiger, leopard, bear, and wolf, with a skill, pluck, and perseverance, beyond all praise. Tell his father he has a bundle of skins of all sorts, but won't send them till he can wrap them round the ivories of a "tusker" elephant. These are rare in the Vindhya near us, and he has not yet had an opportunity. We had a terrible old tiger who had kept out of my way. Our puggees swear it is the same that ate Gopaji's cousin, and Devaji declares he knows by the "pugs" that it is the same that took his child more than a year back. Be that as it may, he will eat man or child no more. Tommy had a squeak for his own life in killing him though; fired my light rifle, which he had in hand, first, and only broke a paw. Had Bikhu bolted, as some gun-bearers will, Tommy's career was ended; but that stout-hearted gallows-bird stood his ground, and handed in the two-ounce in a twinkling. The ball lodged in the brain. Thence Tommy's safety, and Bill Baccy's into the bargain. Thence also the yelling, shouting, drumming, and gong-beating this blessed night. I should explain that Bheel Bikhu is, in Cransdale parlance, "Bill Baccy"—so says Sergeant Wilmot. My love to Lady Cransdale, and to Lady Royston, if she's at Rookenham. Remember me to Keane, when you see him. As for darling mother, love's too little for her—for you, too, so far as that goes—from your ever dutiful and affectionate

NED.

Lokselabad.

Dearest Father,

I wonder whether the name whence I date will ever get on to any map or stick on any. Don't think me guilty of any vanity. I called the town that is to be, and fort that nearly is, Yussuffabad, in honour of Sir Joseph, my chief. But neither actual builders, future burghers, nor expectant garrison of Irregulars, would brook it. He was never within two hundred koss of the place, they insisted; but Locksley Sahib stamped, and behold a fort, a town, a canal, and tanks. So, with a little wrench for euphony, they gifted the foundation with our patronymic, I struggled against it, for I was afraid of the Psalmist's reproach, you know—

"They think that their houses shall continue for ever; and that their dwelling-places shall endure from one generation to another; and call the lands after their own names. Nevertheless, man will not abide in honour; seeing he may be compared to the beasts that perish; this is the way of them. This is their foolishness, and their posterity praise their saying." But remonstrances were in vain; and I am first fortifying, then building, Lockselabad. I had made a big road, as you know, to this extreme point, which some day, I hope—though not, I fear, in mine—may pierce the hills which here come down to the river's bank. But I had no notion of making a road for mere convenience of inroad of freebooters from the hills. Wherefore I planned a fort. But below it, as the hills trend sharp off, lies a plain, which was half desert simply for want of irrigation. There was an old canal; but the sluices were seized by one of the semi-bandit land-owners, of whom I have often written, who, holding in his hands thus the sources of barrenness or plenty, ground down the peasantry at pleasure, till his exactions made them almost all forsake the neighbourhood. Then it was not even worth *his* while to keep the canal in repair. The banks fell in and the channel became a heap of mounds.

Under the guns of my fort no landowner, great or small, bandit or other, could play such pranks. So I stamped—that is, offered good wages—got workers with a will, scooped out the old course, and carried it farther inland, across the plain. Please God, next year we shall stand comparison with the Delta of the Nile itself. There are two or three considerable towns across the river, within the Hon. Company's domains, so that a ferry, still under the guns of my precious pet, the fort, will create a commerce, of which Lockselabad will be the active centre. Of course, I shall institute a fair or two—cattle dealing *versus* cattle stealing, which even my Bheels begin to understand as an advantageous exchange. But for all these blessings I shall have to fight with an ineffable scoundrel, Mundroop Singh. This fellow is a Bheelalah, that is, of mixed parentage, by a Rajpoot father and a Bheel mother. The bad qualities of both races are marvellously combined in him. Proud, fierce, and debauched as a Rajpoot, ignorant, shameless, and thieving, as a Bheel, he is as sanguinary as both. He has long been the terror of the surrounding country, and has hitherto set at defiance the forces of both the native states between which his paternal hill-range intrudes. God willing, when my fort is built, I will have a reckoning with him.

I am gathering quite a little army in a small way. My famous cow-guards, as you know, were bow-and-arrow men; but when I went fort-levelling, as I did last year, preparatory to my fort-building, I was obliged to form a company to the use of fire-arms. Tommy Wilmot is a first-rate light infantry drill, so I have had his somewhat irregular leave on 'urgent tiger-killing affairs' commuted to a sort of permanent non-commissioned commission under me, and he is adjutant to my barefoot Bheels. I have taught him to ride, which he does with pluck, though not much seat or hand. I have a man of men, however, for my irregular horse, who are long since thoroughly organized, equipped, and disciplined. My aide-de-camp, lieutenant, chief of the staff, riding-master—what shall I call him?—is a glorious old Mussulman trooper, an Arab and a Centaur by birth, a sword-grinder by trade, and a swordsman by long practice. He has a capital beard for an Arab—they not being an hirsute race—once black, now grizzling. He has but one eye, "a piercer though," as we used to say at school. His name is Nusreddeen. He has been in most services in India, where there was good riding and hard fighting, never, however, serving long in any, when quiet times came. His last corps was Stubbs'

Irregulars, whence he took his discharge on learning, no one knows how, that I was getting a troop together in these regions. It seems he took a fancy to my management of Rosa Barrington's little peppery gray, which he saw me ride in Bombay, and swore "by Mahomed," that when I should ride afield he would be close behind. I have made him Jemadar, and should the corps increase, he shall be Rissaldar, or chief native officer in due course of time. The one-eyed is a wonderful bigot in most things, except, strange to say, in his theoretical horsemanship, and is quite willing to incorporate some of my "cross-country" notions from Cransdale with the tight curb "haute-école." We make our sowars hunt hog with as much diligence as drill. I am sorry to say the plain which has fallen out of cultivation, below Lockselabad, is only too fine a field for the sport; the old canals and water-courses making pretty jumps. Anything lighter, straighter-riding, and more dashing than our little corps, is, we flatter ourselves, far to seek. Most of our troopers are young native "swells." Cadets; in some instances, "eldest sons," of good Rajpoot families. They bring their own horses; but as every man must have his hobby, I give or advance them money of my own to improve the remounts, so the "cattle" is wonderful well-bred throughout. By the way, I have overdrawn by two or three hundred pounds, giving a bill on you, which shall be duly repaid. I have not been gambling this time, nor even breaking my bank with horse-dealing, as you might imagine; but I have been building a new village or two for some reclaimed Bheels, whose chief, I am sorry to say, I was compelled, after several pardons, to hang. There was no government money available. Those rascals of the durbar or ministry, squandered so much of what we collect, spite of all Sir Joseph can do to check them; so, lest my wild men should take to the woods again if I delayed my promise to provide for them, I made the clearings and built the villages at my own expense. One of the latter had to be rebuilt again—a "rogue" elephant from the Vindhya having trampled its bamboo edifices into splinters one night. Tommy Wilmot avenged the architect. And now I must conclude. Not, however, it strikes me, without informing you what the one-eyed thinks of my grandfather's old regulation sword. He went into fits over it. Vowed that "Shums" itself, to wit Damascus, never forged such a blade. He has ground it and set it to such an edge that I could literally shave with it, had I not long since discarded that effeminate custom. He has made a wonderful wooden scabbard for it, soft "shammy" leather within, and red velvet without. But for the handle no man on earth would assign a "regulation" origin to it.

By the way, the shammy leather is of sambur hide, a large kind of deer, which Tommy or Bikhu shoot for venison, and the latter tans and softens as only savages can. So you see I have good men and true with me, of divers nations, tongues, and peoples. I lead a laborious, active, full, and varied life. I should be sorry to leave or change it, though a run home would be like a peep into Paradise. You know where and to whom to distribute loves and remembrances. Tell the Wilmots that Nusreddeen, who is a great iconoclast, discovered that some of the Bheels make clay-figures of their Tommy, in huge yellow moustaches, with a dead tiger at his feet. I am afraid some of the votive offerings formerly made to Waghia, deceased, are actually made to the image of his slayer. Love of loves to mother.

Your ever dutiful and affectionate

NED.

Bheem Kote in the Hills.

Dearest Father,

It must have been six months or more since I intimated to you my desire to square accounts with Mundroop Singh. Plunderer, ravisher, and murderer as he was, my intention had been to wait till I had finished my fort, obtained some reinforcements from Sir Joseph, made alliance with the native state on the other side of his hills, and drawn a cordon round them. Then, I should have sent in to offer him life and liberty, on condition of his coming in, submitting to the durbar, and emigrating to some fixed, distant, and less dangerous quarter. An audacious and atrocious act of his own has precipitated his fate. Naturally enough he viewed with evil eye the building of my fort at Lockselabad; but the course of its construction, apparently over-awed him. Anyhow he gave no sign, though sinister rumours of his doings on the other slope of his hills would reach us from time to time. It seems, however, that he kept an eye upon our movements. Last week the fort was finished, and I had notice from Sir Joseph that two twelve and four six-pounders, a marvellous park of artillery for this part of the world, had been allotted by the durbar to arm it. The troops from the capital would escort the pieces about two-thirds of the way hither to a small town, called Kallishuhr. There I was to meet them with my squadron, and bring them safe to their destination. I set out on Tuesday, leaving only some half-dozen sowars behind; but a company of the Bheel infantry, and Tommy Wilmot in command. His presence, known by spies to Mundroop, kept that worthy from venturing within rifle-shot of the walls; but my absence with the cavalry gave too tempting an opportunity for a raid to be neglected. On the second morning of my march, that was on the Thursday, he and a rabble of mounted robbers, swept down from the hills across our plain, plundering and burning the villages, and committing outrages too dreadful to name. He reckoned to have gained his fastnesses before intelligence could reach me. But he reckoned without Bikhu, and, above all, without Abool Harg. I had left that vicious but incomparable Arab at home, on account of his propensities to kick and bite at other horses on the march, and pull out picket pegs on bivouac, and trample upon sleeping Syces. But he and Bikhu have an understanding, as I think I have told you before. He is no great rider: but can go on a level. When news came to Wilmot of the mischief raging, he jumped to the wise conclusion that I should have instant news or none. He asked the Bheel whether he could ride the chestnut and overtake me. Bikhu says that he told the horse thereupon what the state of things was. That will seem strange to you; but the horse is a magical creature in the Bheel creed, and rarely have I heard a wild legend round their camp fires in which there did not figure an enchanted steed. Bikhu vows that the Arab understood him, and let himself be saddled like a lamb. Considering the hour at which he and his rider joined us he must have gone like a greyhound when the saddle was on. Before sunrise on Friday we were on our way to pursue the marauder, which I resolved upon at once, sending on a solitary sowar to give news of this diversion to the artillery and its escort. Bikhu was again invaluable. He knew of a jungle path which we could follow in single file, and which led, by a short cut, to the most distant angle of our ravaged plain. We reached it late that evening. We found some of the villagers of its farthest hamlet creeping back to look upon the charred remains of their cottages. That was a rousing sight enough; but will you credit my report—and, crediting, can you conceive my feelings, when these poor people brought me children, with their hands mercilessly severed from their wrists by the swords of those bloodstained ruffians! Mundroop himself had ordered the mutilation: and had said with fiendish laughter that Locksley Sahib was a great "hakeem," and might sew them on again, perhaps!

Saturday's sunrise saw us once more upon the march. The track was easy enough to follow, and was such that we could all perceive the truth of Bikhu's assertion that the homeward ride of the robbers was at footpace and in fancied security.

About nine o'clock in the morning it became evident that we were close upon them. How my blood boiled! I prayed that I might not lose my senses in the excitement, and so fail to bring the matter to righteous and revengeful issue. The bleeding stumps of those poor innocents, whom he had not even Herod's excuse for smiting, seemed to madden me. Presently the Bheel dismounted. He was riding my quieter charger, and was leading the way. I myself rode Abool Harg. Bikhu, motioning to us to halt, laid his ear on the ground. After a long and breathless silence, he declared that he could discern the trample of hoofs a-head. I turned to look upon my troopers: not one but had a grip upon the handle of his sword. We were by this time in a stony ravine, which wound round the base of a hill with a very gradual ascent. One of the peasants, whom the sowars had taken in croup, to act as guides if necessary, assured me that there was open ground almost immediately beyond. On it, then, we should charge the wretches. The wind, which was pretty fresh, was happily whistling down the pass. It carried to them no sound of our approach. When we emerged from it, in utter silence, we were comparatively close upon their heels. At last, one turned and caught sight of us, as we deployed into line, on the edge of the little plateau. Crime upon crime! They had many women with them, dragged from the ruined villages. Some borne before them on their own horses, some upon little hill ponies. Hapless girls! man after man, as he cast his prey loose, cut at the poor creatures savagely with his scimitar. A yell of indignation burst from us—as we rode at them like a whirlwind.

I saw Nusreddeen myself ply his sword among the miscreants with ghastly butchery.

Bikhu, who rode manfully beside me, pointed out a man on a magnificent black horse.

"That is Mundroop!" I had neither eyes, nor heart, nor arm, for any other; but went upon him as on a boar in the open. He saw it and put his horse to his best pace. I knew the breed from the moment I could see his stride. A noble animal, from Kattiwar; but never did Kattiwaree mare drop foal that could get away from a pure Nejd Arab of such rare size, speed, and strength as Abool Harg. I felt we should soon shake off the field, and that Mundroop, at last, must turn and fight me hand to hand, or be ridden down and sabred as a hog is speared. What minutes they were as we stretched out! He at full speed, I keeping my horse in hand, not knowing of what necessity some reserve of wind and power might prove. Fancy settling down to work thus deliberately, in pursuit of the best swordsman on the north bank of Nerbuddah! The excitement was of that kind which gives back all the calm of which the first agitation robs one. I can remember passing my sword into the bridle hand that I might use the right to pat my charger's neck, leaning forward in the stirrups. I should think we must have ridden a mile before he discovered that Abool Harg was not to be blown. He began to save the Kattiwaree. I did not alter my pace for a second, and of course gained on him now at every stride. He pulled up short, throwing the black almost upon his haunches as he wheeled round to confront me. Perhaps he thought I should rush past before I could rein in, and so expose myself to a back-hander. Man and horse had been too well trained at hog for that. To my surprise he threw up his hands, both weaponless, bringing them together with the peculiar supplicating gesture of an Eastern craving quarter. I lowered my point. Quicker than lightning he snatched a pistol from his shawl belt, fired, and threw it at me, seizing his sword, which was hitched naked at his saddle-bow. Abool Harg saved me. The pistol ball I found afterwards had grazed and stung him. He rose up and plunged with a scream at the Kattiwaree, striking out like a demon with his fore hoofs. Master as he was of horse and sword, Mundroop missed his sweep at me. I thrust at him with whatever force an Indian sun has not dried up out of a cricketer's arm, drawing back the razor-like blade after a cutting fashion, which I had learned from Nusreddeen. The mutilated children and their slaughtered mothers were avenged. He sunk forward on his horse's mane and fell heavily to the ground as the animal shied from Abool Harg's renewed assault. Wretched man! It seemed horrible not to dismount and see if any life were left in him to be staunched with the flowing blood. Yet I dared not attempt it: having to battle with my horse, wild to stretch out in pursuit of the other. Two horsemen were nearing me. Half blind with sand and sweat I could not discern whether friend or foe. So I waited, facing them, the fallen man lying close behind my restive horse's heels. The "empty" Kattiwaree made for them. One caught its bridle, which made me think they must be riders of Mundroop's band. I set my teeth, resolving to drive the spurs in and launch myself at full speed against them; but a few moments showed me the well-known figures of Bikhu and the one-eyed Jemadar. I called to the former to jump off and take my Arab's bridle, leaving the two others to Nusreddeen. Then I dismounted; but found the miserable robber chief stone dead. His sword was tightly clenched in his stiffened fingers. I had much ado to release it. You shall have it, dear father, in exchange for that which slew him. Nusreddeen insisted that we must bring the corpse away with us, else it would never be believed what doom had overtaken him. I fastened it therefore,—it was a sickening task,—upon the Jemadar's own beast, he mounting the captured Kattiwaree. The Bheel then remounted and led the troop horse with the ghastly burden. Nusreddeen and I rode after him, side by side; but at respectful distance from each other, my brute still making vicious manifestations as we went. Two of my sowars are killed, six wounded. Nineteen of the robbers are slain, and many wounded. We have four prisoners. I send this letter by an orderly who carries news of the skirmish to the Resident, and a request for the troops at Kallishuhr to march at once with the two six-pounders upon Mundroop's stronghold in the hills. I mean to join them there and rifle the nest at once, now the kite is killed. Not a moment more to spare. Kiss mother for me.

Your ever dutiful and affectionate

NED.

Khanum Bagh.

That is, dear mother, the lady's garden. A romantic place to date from, and a fine romance of real life I have to write from such a place of dating. Well, if I was once refused, I have now made, in my turn, a refusal. If you can't quite say of me—

"He jests at scars that never felt a wound,"

you will think that the wound at which I can afford to jest has at last healed wholesomely. Only think, if an earl's daughter would have none of my wooing, a king's widow has wooed me! I might be sitting on a rajah's musnud and wearing a rajah's puggree—*anglicè*, be throned and turbaned, had I not turned a deaf ear to a Ranee's blandishments. It is fair to say that Koompany Bahawdur don't encourage such escapades on the part of its young "politicals," and had I listened to the voice of the charmer I might have been swinging at a rope's end opposite the Residency; a consideration which *may* have had its influence on my decision. But now for my romance, which nevertheless is a reality.

I must have often told you tales of our Maharanee Lall Beebee, the widow of the last Rajah of this precious principality. She is the mother, or reputed mother, of the sickly child in whose name the durbar rule. Handsome, bold, and witty, she has the reputation of a minor Messalina. Her political intrigues put Sir Joseph out of all patience now-a-days, as her intrigues of another kind used to put the late Rajah out of it. They say she knew precisely when it became imperative to put him out of something more, to save herself, at last. So the lamented sovereign's coffee disagreed with him, although her own fair hands prepared it. I had business at the Residency some few months after Mundroop Singh's affair. By the way, I never heard whether his sword came safe to hand at Cransdale. Be sure you let me know some day. When I was about to leave again, Sir Joseph said to me, that her Highness the Maharanee had asked that I and my Irregulars should escort her, her son, and her ladies, to this country residence of the royal Zenana.

That was fairly in the way of business, my own route lying somewhat in the same direction. Our departure was delayed some few days to meet the views of her Highness's astrologer; but on an auspicious evening the cavalcade set forth, horses and asses, mules and camels, with a sprinkling of elephants. My duty was to see that nothing came in the Maharanee's way, and to keep out of it myself. For two days I succeeded in doing both; on the third Abool Harg interfered to prevent me from doing the latter. He took an obstinate fit just as a sort of palanquin containing the fair lady was coming up a narrow path at the swinging trot of its human beasts of burden. There was some confusion and alarm on their parts as the brute kept plunging, and the curtains being thrown back, by accident or on purpose, I had a full view of the affrighted Maharanee. To do her justice, her fright seemed rather affected than real. I thought her completely collected, and fully capable of bestowing nod, beck, and wreathed smile, amidst her interesting agitation. Perhaps you will say I do her *in*justice. She thought fit, however, to declare that her nerves had received a shock; and as our next camping-ground was in a very pleasant place by a marble shrine and a large tank, with trees in abundance, she refused to stir thence on the ensuing day. I was sitting in the afternoon in my own tent, pitched, as you may imagine, at a wide and respectful distance from that of her Highness—indeed, at the extreme farther angle of the vivifying tank—when one of the wretched nondescript appendages to a female Eastern court entered, announcing himself as her Highness's vukeel or confidential agent. His business, he informed me, was to secure my attendance at a grand "nautch," to be given by the Maharanee in honour of her happy escape. It would be a sumptuous affair. There was a famous troop of dancing girls attached to the tank temple; they would join the ordinary performers of her Highness's retinue.

Now the paganism of the nautch, and the degradation of its poor dancers, have always shamed and disgusted me. I was present at one such entertainment in my early Indian days, and have never chosen to attend another. I, therefore, with what complimentary apologies I could, intimated my disinclination to the vukeel. He was not easy to satisfy, throwing out unambiguous hints of the grief which my refusal would cause his mistress, who, though screened from my observation, was desirous of beholding the features of such a Roostum, such a hero, as the English Sahib who slew Mundroop Singh. The obstinate old ape indeed plied me with so many questions as to my reasons for refusing, that in a sort of exasperation I told him such an entertainment was not according to the law of our Book, nor, if I mistook not, of the Koran itself. The Maharanee, I must tell you, is of a Mussulman house; and I remembered that in Egypt the Almehs, a sort of nautch girls, had been banished, for reformation sake, from the capital, with concurrence of the Moollahs, if not at their suggestion. This rid me of the vukeel, whom I have not set eyes on since. The next morning we resumed our march. During the mid-day halt, a muffled figure, passing quickly by me, slipped into my hand a little scroll of paper. When I could unroll and read it unobserved, I found it to contain two or three Persian sentences, to the effect that as Kadigah's reverence did but increase her affection for the true

Prophet, so might the heart which warmed for a warrior esteem a saint. I took this for a polite sneer from the offended Maharanee, yet was not a little astonished at her attempt to open a correspondence. That astonishment grew, when that same evening Thakali, my Bheel's wife, entered upon a conversation, half of inuendo, half of remonstrance. She was evidently bursting with some secret, and made the most skilful attempts to draw me into questioning herself, and knitting some negotiation. Her simple arts, I need not say, were in vain; yet it caused me annoyance and anxiety to feel that she was exercising them, and to surmise that some one had been tampering with her as a means of access to myself.

Our marches grew daily shorter, for of course we had to regulate them entirely by the caprices of the royal lady, who seemed bent upon lengthening out this journey beyond the limits of mortal patience. Outlandish dainties of cookery and confectionery found continually their way to my table; and by-and-bye another letter was cleverly thrust into my unexpecting and unwilling hand. This was no mere scrap of furtive correspondence, but almost a state paper, a miracle of shamefulness, of craft, and yet of that childish ignorance and fatuity which so often makes the policy of Asiatics inconceivable to the consistent and sober minds of Europeans. It was a direct and open proposal to unite my personal and political destinies with those of the subtle and audacious Ranee. Studded with quotations from amorous Persian poets, and unrestrained avowals of passion, it disclosed the plan of an intrigue for the overthrow of the durbar, the deposition from his nominal authority of her own infant son, and the seizure of supreme power by herself and me. Her talent for managing her own people, with mine for conciliating the half-savage outliers, would come in aid to the resistless force of such "a darling of the sword" as I. My saintliness was such, that I had only to "proclaim the unity" and allow the Prophet, for all Mussulmen to hail me as a Syud or holy chief at once. The Maharanee would be my Zuleika, and I her Yussuf and Roostum in one. Should I accede to this highly practical, if somewhat startling, proposal, I was to signify the gratifying intelligence by mounting Mundroop Singh's black charger instead of the vicious chestnut for two days, wearing a red turban instead of the white folds of muslin which usually protect my head-piece. Means would then be found for closer, more explicit, and delightful communication.

Was the woman mad or mocking?

Two things were certain. I must bestride the chestnut, night, noon, and morning, sending the black Kattiwaree to the farthest rear of the procession, and must forego the luxury of even a clean muslin wrapper round my perplexed and cogitative temples. She would at least interpret these signs as negative.

She did, and was not slow to resent the injury.

It was but yesterday we reached this place. I encamped upon the outskirts of its wide and really beautiful park. Our last march had been rather long and fatiguing. Much as I wished to turn my back for good and all upon her Highness, I could hardly move the escort to-day. There was, besides, the risk of giving a public affront in return for what was of course a secret overture meant to be more than friendly.

Meditation, even under double canvas and thick trees, is thirsty work with the thermometer at ninety-six in the shadiest shade. To cool my reflections upon the best mode of taking leave without discourtesy, or compromising courteousness, I had recourse to a little jar of sherbet, wrapped round with wet towels, and deposited in the least sultry corner. Happily I took not a gulp, but a mere sip; enough, however, to convince me that something more than sugar and milk of almonds flavoured it. I looked about me and perceived that, over a fold of her veil, the dark piercing eyes of Thakali, who was crouching on the ground outside, were fastened eagerly upon me. I called her quietly but firmly. "Thakali, find a little tame monkey and bring it here to me."

I knew there were dozens of them belonging to the camp followers. She came soon back again with one like an impish infant in her arms. I had got a little tin funnel ready, and forcing it between the creature's teeth, too suddenly to let it bite my fingers, poured a liberal dose of my spicy sherbet down its throat. It had a chain round its waist, the other end of which I made fast to a tent pole.

"Sit down there, Thakali, and watch that monkey for me."

She smiled, without an apparent shade of misgiving or of malignity.

Without another word, I turned to a little table on which lay my writing desk, and setting down the jar in front of me, proceeded to write despatches for Sir Joseph. For nearly an hour no sound stirred save the scratching of my pen. At the expiration of that time there was a sort of whining moan from the monkey. I turned to look on it. It shivered, moaned again twice or three times, had a strong spasm, and died.

The horror and astonishment upon the face of Thakali were almost appalling. She sprang to her feet and turned towards me with the wildest gestures of protestation and entreaty. I said nothing.

"Sahib! She swore to me upon her holy book, that it was a love-charm only: as innocent as mother's milk, if only the right man drank it!"

"Who swore that, Thakali?"

"The beautiful Khanum, the Maharanee!"

Then it all came out, with too much honest breathlessness and vehemence to let me doubt the tale, or suspect my poor Bheel friend of any but friendly treachery. The Khanum herself had sent for her, had seen, had spoken with her; had bewitched her with blandishments, and terrified her with threats; had bribed her with smiles and gold, and bound her with oaths, of which the enumeration would fill an index to a book on demonology. Her craft had apparently read the truth of poor Thakali's gratitude and attachment to me, and she had concocted a story which should enlist them upon the side of her own desires. She had told her that an evil wizard had cast upon myself a spell which had chilled the once warm flame wherewith I loved her; that this alone kept back herself and me from the delights of love and the glories of empire. Should I but drink a draught in which a certain magic powder had been dropped, the spell would break, two loving hearts would come together, and our united star of grandeur would arise.

A true woman, Thakali could hardly be supposed, you know, dear mother, to be guiltless of all love for match-making: a true Bheel, she is a devout believer in art-magic. There were the motives, and there—in the shape of the dead monkey—was the deed. I gave poor Thakali to understand most clearly, that, beautiful Khanums or not, she must never think again of interfering in any possible matrimonial engagements for me: that she would rue the day when ever she should open her lips to any human being on this matter, not excepting her trusty Bikhu, his own self: that the sole other condition of pardon must be that she should wrap the deceased in an old shawl and carry the corpse to the Khanum in private, informing her that he had drank the powdered sherbet, which must account for the departure of Locksley Sahib without formal leavetaking. That was last evening. I am writing far on in the night, meaning to march two hours before sunrise. I have not quite finished my despatches for the Resident, and must not dwell much longer upon my personal adventures to yourself.

So Phil has actually his company in the Guards, and with it his Lieutenant-Colonelcy. It will be long before I have any such handle to my name, being only Lieutenant, without the Colonel appended. After all, I have no right to complain: for my career is more anomalous, in soldiering, than his. I haven't set eyes on my regiment, or foot on its parade ground, these years!

You needn't fear any farther freaks of the Maharanee. She has a forgiving disposition when the first fit is off her. Besides which I am far enough out of her reach at Lokselabad, and mean to sip my sherbet cautiously for six months at least. Love and duty to father.

Your own son,

NED.

Lokselabad.

One only line, dear father, to tell you that the current of my life is once more turned—into the long dreamt of channel this time. I shall learn under a great soldier to be a soldier indeed, of some sort. God grant it be the right. Sir Charles

Napier wants irregular cavalry for his coming campaign in Scinde. I am ordered to march for his head-quarters without an hour's unnecessary delay. Some convention of our Government with this semi-independent State allows our services to be at its disposal. Love to mother. No fear of the Maharanee now, you may tell her. If I can find means of despatching letters on the march, I will; but if none come, don't fret, as the possibility is problematical. In haste, your loving and dutiful

NED.

CHAPTER IX.

"HECH, sirs, joost speer at him," quoth Sergeant Macpherson, with a significant jerk of his canny head towards a little sand-mound outside the wall of Sukkur, on which the General, with hands folded behind his back, stood in conversation with a tall, thin, elderly officer and a younger aide-de-camp.

"By all reule he suld na be the man to fight yon hawk-nebbed Baloochs, ye ken. 'Kites dinna pike out kites' een,' they say; and conseeder the neb the chief carries himsel'."

"Shure thin, sargint, I'm thinking it's the hoith of a name they do be givin' your counthry folk."

"What name might ye be soogestin,' Corporal Molony?" said the Scot, after a prickly sort, as if expecting a pluck at the thistle.

"Isn't it Sawnies they do be callin' yez?" inquired the corporal in the most aggravating tone of insinuation.

"Augh'm at a loss to pairceive the fitness o' sic an apellation," retorted Macpherson loftily, yet with rising choler flushing his broad cheek bones.

Corporal Molony raised his voice; it must have reached the sand-heap, as he replied—

"Shure it's none but a Sawny, sargint, wouldn't know the differ atwixt kites and an aigle. Jist take another look at the Giniral's 'bake' agin, will yez?"

He tapped his own nose, conspicuous for a simous absence of convex curvature, with such inimitable drollery, that even the wrathful Caledonian joined in the guffaw.

The officers could not resist; but turned aside to hide their amusement.

"Did you hear that saucy rascal, Blunt?" asked Sir Charles.

"Oh, hear him! I hear too much of him," answered the Colonel. "He is a corporal of my own light company, and always 'a skrimmaging wid his tongue,' to use his own expression."

"Looks as if he'd skirmish with some other weapon too," said the aide-de-camp.

"True for you," replied the Colonel; "he's a smart enough soldier."

There was not much wind that evening; but what there was blew from the desert. The air was thick with a sandy haze, narrowing the horizon, and rendering objects even at little distance, almost as indistinct as in an English fog. This sort of mist was thickened in one direction by a column of rising dust. Out of it, by degrees, emerged the leading files of a small body of mounted men.

"Well horsed!" observed the General peering through his spectacles. "Serviceable uniform and equipment. Bless me, what a few baggage ponies! What I like to see! Know the corps?" he asked, impatiently, of the aide-de-camp.

"No, Sir."

"Tell the officer in command to halt his men and speak with me."

"What's your name, sir; and what force is that?"

"Locksley, General; Irregulars from the Trans-Nerbuddah."

"Who raised and equipped them?"

"I had that honour, General."

"You seem to have done it well, sir. Is that your usual amount of baggage?"

"I can't easily make it less, Sir; but I am particular about it."

"Right, sir—quite right. The things are well slung too. M'Murdo must see these ponies."

"Your voice seems to come back to me, sir," now said the tall thin Colonel. "Did I understand you to say your name was Locksley?"

"Ned Locksley, Colonel, at your service. Can't you mind the seamews on the Skerry?"

"Good Heavens, my dear boy!" cried the old soldier, in ecstasy, seizing one hand in both his own. "The turban and the beard deceived me. He is a chip of a good old block, Sir Charles. You remember Locksley of the Welsh Rangers?"

"Killed at Corunna, poor fellow?"

"The same. This Ned is his grandson. Let me beg your favourable regard for him."

"His baggage ponies have been beforehand with you, Colonel. Your grandfather was a fine soldier, sir, and I am pleased to make your acquaintance. Come and dine with me when you've seen your men to their quarters. Know Captain Annesley? I dare say he'll show you the Quartermaster-General's."

Ned and the aide-de-camp went their way, their elders returning slowly in another direction.

Having filled, so long, a post of duty so remote, Ned would have been a stranger among his comrades, had it not been for this meeting with Colonel Blunt. O'Brien was the only man of his own standing serving with Napier's small but admirable force. But the old Peninsular was a universal favourite throughout it, known, esteemed, and almost loved by all. His friendship was a passport not only to the chief's acquaintance, but to that of every officer in camp. Ned found himself in double sense at home. At home in the ready brotherhood of his brother officers; at home in the home-memories of the fatherly veteran.

"I was old Ned Locksley's recruit, my boy, and, by George, you are mine. You'd have been a college Don by this time, I believe, but for my 'listing you at Freshet. You should have taken the Queen's shilling though, you young dog, instead of John Company's."

"You know, Colonel, I said if I ever went soldiering, it should be soldiering in earnest."

"Yes, and sarve your impudence right, you've been thief catching and cow-keeping ever since, you see."

Ned laughed. "We shall see soldiering now, sir, I hope, at all events."

"Who'll show it you? One of old Sir John Moore's boys, at last, to say nothing of old Blunt and his Queen's Light Borderers."

"No nobler tutors, Colonel. They can count on an admiring pupil. Is that the Brunswicker's book under your surtout? I think I see the stumpy square outline still."

"By George, boy! So you remember that, do you? Yes, that's my devotional orderly book, as ever. 'Muss oft gelesen seyn.' Eh?"

"I owe you more for that bit of insight, Colonel, into what a soldier's mind might be, than I could make words to tell. I've tried to follow that regulation clause of it myself you see."

Out of the looser folds of his half eastern military tunic he took his little Testament and tendered it to the old officer.

"Thank God for that, Ned!" said he, reverently. "It's better than the Brunswicker, since it is the Word itself. But the Greek beats me. 'I warn't never no scholard to brag on,' and found the Latin tough enough till I got on good terms with it. All right! Come in!"

It was Captain Annesley, to say that the Trans-Nerbuddahs were to parade at daylight.

"He wants to pick a few likely nags and men

for some diversion he is brooding. A march into the desert, I believe, or some such hopeful feat. There ain't a vulture there, I'm told, to pick a fellow's bones, even."

"But they bleach nicely," said the Colonel. "I lost a few poor fellows three marches out of Aden once, and know the sort of thing."

"Well, good night, gentlemen. I needn't say the chief's a punctual party, Mr. Locksley."

It was for the march to Emaumghur, that unparalleled act of happy daring, that the great soldier was picking troopers. Two hundred horsemen only were to escort into the waste less than four hundred infantry, mounted for the nonce on camels. Ned's heart bounded within him as, one by one, the eagle-eyed veteran selected five-and-twenty of his men for service.

"Selection good?" he asked of Locksley when they had formed a line a little in advance of their chafing comrades.

Ned went very carefully down it, only halting at one trooper on a showy looking horse.

"The man's thoroughly good, General; but the horse is not equal to its appearance."

"Pick out a sounder, then."

Ned obeyed. As the proud Rajpoot horseman

learnt his rejection, a tear of rage and disappointment rose to his eyes. The General's glance observed it. Master of every chord which thrilled in a soldier's breast, of whatever race or creed, he said to Locksley—

"Make it clear to your sowar that we pass him over for the horse's fault alone. Tell him I know a man when I see one; and he shall be my orderly the first great fight."

The swarthy features were radiant again at once. The Rajpoot drew his sword and kissed it in token of unalterable fidelity.

"We march at sundown from Emaumghur," then said the General, "I make no secret of it; but have sent on to warn and threaten the Ameer."

A heavy march it was, in the dark night and deep sand. An awful march, next day, under the scorching sun. No forage, and scanty water, at the camping ground when night fell. Even two hundred horse were a hundred and fifty more than the desperate adventure would allow. Yet after that second sifting, when two-thirds of the cavalry were sent back, fourteen of the Trans-Nerbuddahs remained, inclusive of the one-eyed Jemadar and exclusive of their leader, Ned. Strange magic of a manly mastermind! Under a Napier that weary march in the howling wilderness was like a martial holiday. When the very camels grew faint for want of such poor prickly herbage as would satisfy their patient hunger, there was an amicable struggle between the horsemen and the undaunted infantry, for the honour of hauling up the sand steeps the dragging howitzers. For at one time the sand stood heaped and hardened almost into stone, stretching into table lands or stiffening abrubtly into ridges; at another, it swept, with mingled shells and pebbles, as if a rapidly receding tide had left it, round thin streaks of vegetation where the gazelles found covert and the wild boars a lair. Out of one such scrubby mockery of a jungle emerged, one afternoon, to Ned's amusement, the garrulous Molony, holding at arm's length a stick, in the cleft end of which a snake was wriggling.

"Yon's a rare opheedian ye've captured, corporal!" said Macpherson, who had once done hospital-sergeant's duty, and affected scientific phrase.

"O'Fidderan, is it, thin? Sorra the morsel more than Macpherson. The O'Fidderans is no varmint; but dacent folk, near Mallow, mee own cousins, by the mother's side. O'Fidderan, indeed!"

"Augh'm nae desirous o' geevin' offence, corporal; but that's the pheelosophers' name for serpents."

"More's the shame for thim, miscallin' o' craythurs. Couldn't they spell 'snake,' that they'd write O'Fidderan short for sarpint?"

"Ony rate, yon's a vara curious specimen. Ye'll maybe let the foreign doctor have it?"

"Furrin docthor, indeed! Wid his name Mac something. That's a quare way to back a counthryman, Misther Macpherson!"

"Hoot, man! Maximeelian's the gentleman's name, which is nae name of ony Scottish clan. Augh misdoot he's a Gerrman."

Max Gervinus was, indeed, a thorough Teuton. Blue-eyed and fair-haired, tall, stout, and handsome, he had in nowise degenerated from such ancestors as Tacitus drew. His mental was in no ridiculous disproportion to his physical stature. He might have been a man of mark in public life, but for his birth, as subject of a petty state, where cumbrous artificial restraints cramped all political activity within boundaries naturally very narrow; where military life offered no prize beyond the command of a small contingent, rarely called into permanent much less, into active existence; and where commercial enterprise itself could scarcely swell beyond the limits of a larger pedlaring. Too practical to float into the atmosphere of vague metaphysical abstractions, his mind, which yet partook of the speculative German temper, had launched itself upon the sea of physical research and study. Surgeon and physician, he was a chemist, a botanist, and a natural historian. Anxious to enlarge, not in mere theory, his field of view, he had solicited and obtained the post of personal medical attendant to a Serene Highness, of royal German blood, whose spirit, half military and half philosophical, was sending him upon what he himself was pleased to designate a comprehensive-objective politico-material world's-observation-tour. Whatever may have been the genuineness of the philosophical element in his Serenity's composition, there was a fine full dash of Hussar blood in his veins; and the gathering of Napier's force had attracted him irresistibly to Scinde. He had fruitlessly solicited leave to accompany the flying column into the wilderness, though volunteering for the storming party when the stronghold should be reached. But "medicos" being few, and Max covenanting to find his own water, and to act under orders as might any British assistant-surgeon, he obtained the favour denied to his Serene patron, and was permitted, in the interests of science, to risk his life in that noble fellowship. There were two varieties of land-lizard, he assured Ned Locksley, with five of sand-beetle, to be found in the Scindian desert, the securing of which, or of any of which, would amply repay him for any danger encountered or hardship endured. But his language and bearing made it evident to all that he was no mere crackbrained enthusiastic sciolist. His childlike simplicity took nothing from his vigorous manliness, whilst his intellectual accomplishments graced without overshadowing his transparent amiability. He spoke English very fairly, with so few peculiarities, that the canny Macpherson, while dubbing him the "foreign doctor,' showed only characteristic caution in "misdoubting" of his national origin. Ned was charmed with him, with his mingled erudition and acuteness, with his conjectures and questions concerning men or beasts in the remoter hill-tracts and jungles. Long before Emaumghur was reached, they were fast friends. That kite's nest was empty, as all men know, before the eagle's talons could claw the occupants. Nothing remained to do but to make the sticks fly, and take wing backward, as if by scent of water, to the shifting banks of the Indus flood again. The Trans-Nerbuddahs who had not been selected, those also who were sent back on the desert march, were all somewhat consoled on learning that there had been no fight after all. But Nusreddeen was right to see to the grinding and setting of every sword throughout the squadron. Meeanee was at hand.

CHAPTER X.

THAT bloody field was won. The first cares had been given to the wounded, the last offices to the dead. In bestowing the former, on the field itself and in the camp-hospital, Max Gervinus had won golden opinions. He was voted as fine a fellow in his own way as the Serene hussar in his, whose cool and intrepid bearing on the General's staff had been the admiration of the army.

A group of those whom the fresh-hearted though fiery veteran delighted to call "his boys," were clustered in and about his tent, bringing reports or taking orders, recalling the incidents of the terrible day and commenting upon the gossip of the camp. The German medico was hail-fellow with them all, as might be gathered from the frequent interpellations addressed to "Max, my boy."

"I say, Max, old fellow, is it true that his Serenity was hit by a spent matchlock ball?"

"You, Max, there, the chief wants the return of the Borderer's surgeon. Brigadier Blunt says it was given to you to put in. Hand it over."

"Lend us a whiff of your meerschaum, Max, if not in immediate use. My stomach's had fighting enough for one bout, and craves the calumet of peace."

"Max, my boy," said Captain Annesley, "the General wants to know whether you saw that mad thing of Locksley's with Paddy O'Brien. Some one said you could tell him all about it. Come along in then, and let him have it."

"Yes, mine General," answered the young German to the question, when once more put to him inside the tent, "I have seen this ride-and-arms-feat of Mr. Locksley and the Irish officer. It was herrlich, very fine, to see. There was a mass of Beloochs behind one great dry river-bank. They had—how do you say?—scarped it, and made almost a fort. In front was the old river-bed, like a deep dry ditch, along which it must be marched to attack. In once place, the opposite bank which falls everywhere else away makes a kind of promontory, a narrow platform hanging over the Beloochs, with a broad gap, I think you call it, and a very high drop. Two infantry-companies will storm the bank, coming along the river-course, under the old Brigadier-Colonel, with name Blunt, I believe. Mr. Locksley had his men dismounted, a little way from our bank, waiting for the Colonel Pattle's orders. It were two wounded, and I did for them as I could. Mr. O'Brien rode up on a fine gray horse. They shake hands. By-and-by Mr. Locksley shows him the infantry advancing along the dry torrent. Then he points out the platform and says something. O'Brien laughed, and answered how I could not quite understand; something about a boy of soup: no, not soup, the other word, eh?"

"Said he was a 'broth of a boy,' perhaps?" suggested Annesley, amidst general laughter.

"Ah, yes; just so, mine General, he said he was a boy of broth; then they both spoke with that old one-eyed horseman, Nusreddeen. They asked for three volunteers. All the squadron would go. Mr. Locksley said there was no room for more to ride. They fix their saddles and take rank. Mr. Locksley, on his red horse, at the widest place; then Mr. O'Brien, Nusreddeen, and the three Rajpoots. Just when the infantry column reached the redoubt-bank, Mr. Locksley cried 'charge!' Mr. O'Brien 'hurroo!' and the troopers 'wallah!' It is not to believe how they rushed and sprung the cliff over. I ran on foot to the edge and saw them fallen in one plump among the Beloochs. With that the infantry made an effort to crown the parapet. It opened all for them. Good Himmel! that was a thing to see!"

"A daring deed, sir!" said the chief, with kindling eye. "The fruit of combination of character in war. A crack-brained Irish adjutant of infantry, a sober Englishman—half-quaker some one said—and four bold riders of Mussulman horse! How many killed and wounded?"

"One sowar of each," answered Annesley. "Paddy O'Brien has broken his right collar-bone, and the one-eyed Jemadar has an ugly gash on the forehead, but not dangerous."

"Did nothing happen to Locksley then, himself?"

"Not a scratch; but his horse was killed."

"What, that vicious chestnut?" asked some one. "He was a fine brute."

Even so. Poor Abool Harg's carcase feasted the Scindian vultures; and, soon after Hyderabad was fought, the rising waters swept his bones away.

Before that second day of Scindian slaughter, the prize which he had helped to win for his master, the black Kattiwaree, had a busy time of it. Now scouring the Shikargahs to dislodge lurking bodies of the Ameer's cavalry, now riding long and dangerous stretches almost across the line of Shere Mohamed's army, to communicate with reinforcements on the march from above.

Ned had scarcely a day unoccupied of all the month and more which intervened between the two great fights. His Serenity had a lazy fit, a subjective-philosophical being's-phase, as he would have it after the hot struggle at Meeanee; lying upon a divan in Hyderabad itself, imbibing such cool drinks as were procurable, and making a moonshee read the Shastras with him. Max was free to ride up and down with the Trans-Nerbuddahs, and availed himself of the privilege to the utmost. Spite of the reverence wherewith the One-eyed looked upon a "hakeem" of the Feringhees, that grim swordsman beheld him with a suspicion, which even the success of his styptics on his tulwar-cut could not remove at first. The dried herbs, the corked beetles, the skinned snakes, and the bottled lizards, seemed to point to nefárious arts. Nusreddeen, with some hesitation, as if treading consciously on delicate ground, went so far as to ask of his commander, whether it was for fear or favour that the Sahib-log got on such easy terms with magicians like that young hakeem, and whether he, the commandant, was not in nightly fear of afreets, with such a brother of evil spirits to sleep in the tent with him. But a scuffle which took place in an out-lying village, one fine evening, stopped all his scruples. Max was no Centaur—your central German rarely is—but he had been president and champion of a sword-club, at his own university. It was all the worse, therefore, for the Lugaree tribesman who set upon him, that he was afoot and armed with a straight German blade. At least it would have been, but for Max's perfect good-humour, who contented himself with slicing his adversary's wrist, making him drop his tulwar like a live coal.

His quick and quiet skill won the sword-grinder's heart. Magician or not, such a performer with the weapon was thenceforth secure of his admiration and esteem.

But now Major Stack's column, from Muttaree, had effected its perilous junction. Upwards from Kurrachee, downwards from Sukkur, the flotillas, which brought reinforcements by the Indus, had all safely reached head-quarters. Five thousand fighting men were under arms in the British camp outside Hyderabad. Man and beast were resting to gain vigour for the coming shock.

Spite of all means and appliances against the scorching heat, the thermometer had stood at 130° in Brigadier Blunt's tent that day. It was now cooler: moisture from the river rising towards sundown abated the fiery breath of Indian day.

Ned and Max were both in the old soldier's tent. The former in Sybaritic luxury, stretched out on two bullock-trunks, the latter in a camp-chair skinning a lizard with a pen-knife. The Brigadier was absent, in attendance upon the chief, who was giving his final directions. When he came in, he unbuttoned his uniform coat and threw it across the tent towards his bed. His little book dropt out. Max, with ready good-nature, jumped off his chair to pick it up. His eye caught the writing on the fly-leaf.

"Pardon me, mine Brigadier. Dare I then ask you where you became—ah, I always make that mistake—I mean where you did get this little book?"

"I took it from a dead man's hand upon the field of Waterloo."

"Dare I then look at it again?"

"By all means. What strikes you, Max, about it? I believe the little manual is common enough in Germany."

"Yes; but this handwriting, this name of Gretli Steiner! Tell me, mine Brigadier, do you remember what for a man that was from whom you took it?"

"A strapping fine fellow. A death's-head Brunswicker."

"Ah, then, the book was her's My good Aunt Grettel! How wonderful is this!"

There was a quaver in Max's voice as he gave way to this exclamation, and something very like a tear in his big blue eye.

Ned sat bolt upright on the bullock-trunks to stare at him, and the war-beaten features of the old Brigadier were troubled.

"My good aunt, Grettel. Yes! That was her love, her life, that death's-head Brunswicker. Her bride-clothes were made when he must join the regiment. She never wore them till they put her in her coffin, not five years back. I saw her lie dressed out in them. She was just as my mother, was Aunt Grettel. My mother died before I can remember. You will forgive me, mine Brigadier!"

And the big round drops, from which he tendered

his apology, came brimming over. Neither elder nor younger soldier found a word. So Max laid down the book and took to skinning the lizard again, opening out his heart to the two stranger-comrades whose silence carried sympathy.

"Yes, my mother died; so did my father; so did, later, my little sister Lieschen. But Marguerite Steiner, Gretli,, as you say, Maggy, my mother's sister, she did nurse, and feed, and educate me. Ah, that was an heaven's woman, Aunt Grettel! So still, and thin, and white; but then so liebensvoll —what is it? such loving heart.

"One day when I was a spitz bube, a little fool-boy, eh? I asked her so: 'Aunt Grettel, why have you no husband like Frau Mandelheim, your friend, or Frau Tischling, the pastor's wife, or the other ladies whom we know?'

"'I had one, my brave Max,' she said, 'but the Father in heaven wanted his life for the fatherland on earth, and I must spare him; so he went to the war and came to me therefrom never more.'

"She counted him her husband, you see, because they were vertraut, promised, engaged; but yet not married. She had a picture of him in a black frame, with a little silver skull and cross-bones. It hung over a little Dresden vase, which one of his sisters had given her. No flowers but the myosotis were ever put in it. You call that in English, as we do, the 'Forget-mine-not,' eh?"

The lizard was skinned by this time. Max rose and went out, saying, "I will rub in arsenic soap."

Ned stretched himself upon the bullock-trunks again. The Brigadier sat in his camp chair, with the Brunswicker's book open at the place where the blood-spot rusted. After a long pause, he said—

"Max must have it. My use of it is out."

"He is too good a fellow," answered Ned, "to deprive you of what you have used so well, and prized so long."

"That may be. But a man must make restitution before he closes his accounts. I shall not carry this book into the field to-morrow."

"Don't say so, Brigadier. I'm sure Max would be very sorry"—

"It's the ould one-eyed Jimadhar would have word of Misther Locksley, yer 'onour, outside," said Molony, appearing with a salute at the veteran's elbow.

"I thought we had been too long quiet," observed his younger comrade, buckling on his sword, and offering his hand to the old Colonel.

"Good night, if I shouldn't see you again."

"Good night, my dear good fellow. God in heaven bless you. Good night, Ned;" and he wrung his hand with an unusual force.

"Meanin' no offince, yer 'onour," ventured Molony, as Ned passed out from the tent; "it's yerself would maybe spake a word for uz to the Ordnance Sthorekeeper?"

"What on earth do you want of him, corporal?"

"Sarjint, plase yer 'onour. And its thanks to yerself it is."

The corporal had won his promotion where Abool Harg's bones lay bleaching.

"I'm heartily glad to hear it," Locksley said. "But what do you want of the Storekeeper?"

"Iv he'ud plase to sarve uz out stout umberellas a-piece, it might be useful to uz Light Borderers."

"What? For the sun? It won't rain to-morrow, sergeant, you may take your affidavit."

"Ah now, yer 'onour, maybe t'would rain 'irrighular khavilry?' Sure an' it did the last time! Worse than 'cats and dogs, and pitchforks.' By the same token, thim's the marks of yer iligant hunter's hoofs on me schako."

He tendered the head-piece for closer inspection. Both laughed heartily.

"A miss is as good as a mile, sergeant, so good night to ye," said Ned, rejoining Nusreddeen, and making with him for the quarters of the Trans-Nerbuddahs.

Their place in the next day's line was on the British left, in support of Leslie's dashing horse-artillery. Thus, when the cavalry of that wing came scrambling twice across the Fullaillee river, through the scrubby jungle on its farther banks, and with spurs deep in their horses' sides, clearing the nullahs in front of the village of Dubba, they were among the foremost of the reckless chargers who forced their way into its outskirts, among houses carefully loopholed and swarming with matchlock men.

The contemplation-phase of his Serenity had fled with the shrill bugle-call that had forewarned the dawn of that fierce encounter. He and his little suite, Max in the midst of them, were at that crisis well up with Ned and his leading sowars. An abbatis of trees and prickly bush checked, however, their headlong assault in one of the village lanes. Max and his Highness were out of the saddle as quickly as Ned himself and the most active of his horsemen, tearing away with frantic energy at the provoking obstacle. On their left they could hear the trampling gallop, and victorious cry of the squadrons who had ridden clear of this entangling lane; on their right, the crash of musketry, the mingled roar and shriek of grim and desperate contest kept ever increasing. But the surging tide of Napier's war was rolling back the forces of the enemy. Red-coated Sepoys came swarming over the mud-wall and joined themselves to the troopers in the effort to clear the way. Ned thought that one of them had hailed himself as "Locksley Sahib!" with a shout of exultation. The sticks and branches at his corner were almost cleared. He was trying to coax the Kattiwaree, who had turned shy and restive, across a fallen truuk, too heavy to be lifted. At that instant there was a cry of "Allah! Allah! Deen! Deen!" and a band of devoted fanatics, sworn to die in massacring the infidel, rushed out of a dwelling-house immediately at hand. His back was turned and his sword dangling at his wrist. Nothing could have saved him, but the devoted sacrifice of the strange Sepoy, who had shouted out his name. The lad—he was a mere boy, indeed, and wore a drummer's uniform—without attempting any stroke of self-defence, sprang with outstretched arms between the English officer and his assailants, whose tulwars gashed his body with a dozen cruel wounds. Locksley was untouched, but the blades of the sword-grinder and of his troopers were already red with vengeance on the "Ghazees" that would have slain their leader.

"Max! In the name of mercy, see to this poor lad for me. I must push on."

At the word, he was in the saddle again, and galloping forward with his men.

Some of the camp followers, who already scented victory and possible plunder, were not far off. His Highness, who like the rest there present, had seen the boy's admirable devotion, and who was generous as becomes a man of his rank, bribed them with promise of a handful of rupees, to sling a sort of impromptu dhoolie and bear him to the rear as soon as Max had done all that he might upon the spot, to secure him against bleeding to death of his ghastly wounds.

The villages and lanes beyond Dubba, with the nullahs which had been vain to protect it were gorged with dead and dying. The tent-pitchers, therefore, grass-cutters, syces, and the like, received orders to encamp almost upon the ground which the army had occupied before the action began. When Ned returned thither, some four or five hours afterwards, he found his tent-bed occupied by the wounded drummer, in close attendance on whom sat Max Gervinus.

"Shall you save him, Max?"

He shook his head doubtfully.

"Is he sensible?"

"I can hardly say. He lies so very still."

But the boy hearing voices, though he knew no English, turned towards them; and seeing Ned, said in Hindustani, audibly, though feebly—

"You will bear me witness, Sahib, I have paid the debt."

"What debt, my brave boy? It is I owe you one, that will be hard to pay. You gave your life for mine."

"What a father owes, a son owes," answered the lad, with a shiver, that Max noted anxiously.

Ned had no notion of his meaning; but the words smote with strange familiarity upon his ear. They carried him back in instantaneous vision into the by-gone time, far away from the scorched plain of slaughter. His own father, Robert Locksley, trod the green lawn from Cransdale House towards the Lodge, and he himself, a curly-headed boy, went side by side with him, watching the play of sunlight between the waving outspread of the cedars, and uttering the same words which had fallen from the bleaching lips of the dark Hindoo lad.

"Promise me, Sahib," he resumed, "that you will let my father know."

"Who is your father, my dear boy? Where does he live? And tell me exactly what you would have him know."

"Let him know that I saved from the Ghazees the Sahib who treated him like a brother Christian."

Then little by little the story was gathered.

The lad's father was the man whose master had mocked at his profession of faith before assembled guests, and whose hand Ned Locksley, by a generous impulse, had taken in his own with honour.

The young ensign's name had been thenceforth a household word of joy and pride with him. When the regiment, in the band of which the lad was drummer, was ordered upon service, Panjerah, who had contrived to learn that Ned was now a commandant of horse, had charged his son most solemnly to find out Locksley Sahib, properly of the Bombay Europeans, and to prove his gratitude by word or deed.

Nobly had he done his father's bidding. Poor lad! He said he was a Christian, too, in answer to

Ned's questioning upon the point. "Not such a good one as my father, Sahib!" Ned would not tell him, fearful of misleading a soul fast ebbing out of life, how splendid a confirmation his own action was of the Great Master's word: that there are "last which shall be first." Yet he spoke to him of that Great Master—spoke of him as the Pardoner—spoke of him as the Captain of Salvation; and so the name of names was on the lips of the boy-hero, when, before midnight, his last syllable was breathed.

Day had scarcely broken when Locksley left his tent again. Outside, crouching over a camp fire with the One-eyed, sat the Irish sergeant. A grasscutter had just thrown on an armful of dry canes, which blazed up red and glaring. The sergeant rose and saluted. By his countenance, Ned knew that his tidings were heavy.

"I hope to Heaven the Brigadier is not hurt, Molony?"

"Niver was a sweeter corpse to look upon, yer 'onour," was the too significant answer.

Strange to say, no hint of the calamity had reached the younger officer in hurried sentences exchanged with comrades, yesterday, on the return from arduous pursuit. The shock was great, even to nerves strung for such sights and sounds as soldiers face with manliest resolution.

"Lord rist his sowl!" said the Irishman; "he was a grand soldhier, inthirely. 'Tis a bitter black day for the Queen's Light Borderers!"

"Not a man in this army will dispute it, sergeant. Where is he hit?"

"Behind the right ear yer 'onour. He marched up a big bank, and looked over as cool as a cow-cumber. 'Quick wid yez, boys,' he ses, 'it's full o' thim!' They let fly their matchlocks, and back he fell, dead, amongst us, the sowl."

"Where is he, sergeant?"

"In his own tint, shure, laid out bheautiful."

Ned followed him, and found what the Irish soldier thus insisted on, quite true. The expression was painless, almost smiling, not defiantly, as some younger warrior might smile at death in battle, but quietly and wistfully, as a veteran might smile on the brave lads whom he was calling up the deadly steep. The quick and tender penetration of the Celt had read it right.

"Shure, that was his look always, yer 'onour, whin the rigiment had its work cut out for it. Sorra the Cornel iver loved his boys betther."

The genuine warmth with which he spoke,

thawed for a moment the reserve of British discipline. Ned laid his hand on Molony's shoulder, and said:

"You are a fine fellow, sergeant. An officer may be proud to lead such lads."

"Faix it was foiner than gittin a meddhal, Misther Macpherson," was his own commentary on the condescension, when talking it over with the Scotchman, later.

At the time, however, he only made a formal military salute, taking out of his inner breast-pocket a large square paper, inscribed by the Brigadier's own hand—for Edward Locksley, Esq., Bombay Europeans, Commanding Trans-Nerbuddah Irregular Horse.

When the seal was broken, Ned found it to contain a small packet of documents and vouchers, tied with red tape; a paper marked, "my will," and a note with his own name upon it.

"Dear Ned,

"I have got 'the route' this evening, and do not look to march back from the field to-morrow. Tell Max I shall give his love to Grettel and the Brunswicker, if, as I hope and believe, I come across them in those quiet cantonments. I have neither chick nor child, brother nor sister, so I do no man injustice in leaving you my goods and chattels, pay and prize money; partly for your grandfather's sake, still more for your own. Cox and Co. are the regimental agents, and know all about my affairs. You'll find them in strict order, I believe. Good-bye, Ned, and God bless you.

"Your old friend,

"JOHN BLUNT,

"Brigadier Colonel-Commanding, Q. L. B."

Under this touching proof of personal affection Ned broke down, threw himself into the camp-chair, and fairly sobbed. The sergeant, with innate delicacy, stepped out forthwith, leaving him alone with the dear old Brigadier.

By-and-by came officers of the Light Borderers, whom imperative necessities had hitherto kept absent. Few enough they were to discharge the most urgent military duties on the morrow of a fight, in whose thickest and deadliest fray the flower of their admirable regiment had gone down before the scythe of Death. Not knowing what scant time might be theirs for formalities or ceremony, the will was opened in their presence. It was, as Ned's letter announced, a simple declaration that the old Colonel left him his universal legatee, with charge to let each regimental officer have some useful keepsake from the campaigning kit, and to restore the Brunswicker's prayer-book to Max Gervinus, with fifty guineas to buy a mourning ring. Soon after, came the Chief himself, to take a last look at his old Peninsular comrade, and to provide that the victorious army should honour his burial with such military pomp as the short halting time allowed. For infantry drums were already rolling, whilst bugles called the troopers to indefatigable advance.

CHAPTER XI.

"WHAT's all that signalling from the Admiralty flag-staff?" asked Lord Royston of his secretary. "Fleet not going to sea just yet again?"

"Oh, dear no! It's the mail from Alexandria. Broken a shaft or something, and the Admiral ordering out the 'Firebrand' to fetch her in."

It was early in the autumn. Furious equinoctial gales had swept the Mediterranean; but its purple waves dash laughter after tempest against the glowing rock of Malta.

The government of that dependency was an office scarcely compatible with the position to which the former Under-Secretary of State had risen. But the home authorities had begged of him to undertake the introduction of certain changes and reforms, which would come with fuller grace from a statesman having occupied a seat in the Cabinet. Lady Royston, moreover, was a little anxious about the health of her third child—another Constance—and had thrown her whole influence into the scale of accepting a charge, which, without relinquishment of public duty, would secure a winter under a southern sky. The request and determination had alike been sudden. Ned Locksley, standing with Max Gervinus on the paddle-box, to make out with a spy-glass what craft came dashing out to meet them from Valetta, had little thought towards what meeting H.M. steam-sloop 'Firebrand' was come to tow him. As little had Lady Royston and her husband of what friend the broken down "overland" was bringing to the Palazzo; for Ned's run home was unexpected and unannounced.

The Scindian sun had stricken him down one day on his return to Hyderabad, from a successful raid upon the robber tribes. Nusreddeen had carried him at once into the city, where Max was still in attendance upon the German prince. Bled in both arms, he had a short sharp struggle for life, and won it. But the British medical officers joined with Max in forbidding him from getting too soon into the saddle again. The Chief himself, who took much interest in him, was peremptory. He, indeed, it was who insisted upon, rather than suggested, a short trip home. A steamer of the Honourable Company's Navy was at Kurrachee, in which his Serene Highness was to have passage with his suite to Suez. There they would fall in with the mail. What could fit better? As for the Trans-Nerbuddahs, O'Brien, who was long since about again, should have temporary command, for which, his performance in their company at Meeanee had shown him to have considerable dispositions. At Alexandria, the Prince embarked in an Austrian man-of-war for Trieste. Max, who had now fulfilled his charge, accepted Locksley's pressing invitation to accompany himself to England, by way of Malta and Gibraltar.

The 'Oriental,' which had brought them to the island, had left Egypt with a clean bill of health. She was no sooner, therefore, moored in the still harbour of the quarantine, than "free pratique" was granted, and her passengers might disembark.

As they landed at the Marsa-Musette, and strolled up the broad stone steps, a great printed sheet of paper, headed by the Queen's Arms, and pasted against a side wall, was noticed by Max Gervinus.

"Let me see, mine good fellow, what for a Government's proclamation is that?"

But as soon as Ned's eye rested on it, the signature at the bottom drew his attention.

"Royston! Royston! Malta, September the third, Royston, and no Christian name! It must be his!"

"Whose, mine good fellow? Whose what?"

"His signature. The governor's—whom I take to be an old acquaintance."

"Bravo then!" added Max. "We shall have fallen well, with friends at Court, till the steamer mends her machine."

At the hotel in the Strada Reale the landlord at once removed all doubt.

"Yes, Lord Royston—the same who was member of the Cabinet, now represented her Majesty in Malta. It was six weeks since he came out. Lady Royston and their illustrious family were also here."

Being the man he was, Locksley's impatience to see Lady Royston was quite healthy. The true and tender memories of boyhood were what he longed to look for on her noble countenance—not the false dreams, however tender, of his youth.

Within two hours he presented himself at the Palazzo.

"His lordship was engaged with the members of the municipality. Her ladyship was at home, but this was not an usual hour of reception."

On his card he wrote in pencil—"Half-way home to Cransdale."

"Her ladyship might, perhaps, waive her rule for once."

The gilt ceiling of the grand saloon in which the servant left him was emblazoned with the eight-pointed cross of Malta. Its walls held full-length portraits of Grand-masters who had here swayed the power of the sovereign order of St. John. Their histories had often been of kin to his. Some clouds upon the rosy skies of youthful fancy, some lining of those darkling vapours with redder glare of war-like longings, had oftentimes first sent such men as these into a willing exile. He, like them, had heard the war-cry of the unbeliever. He, too, upon a tilting field of desert sand, had felt sword clash with scimitar. He, too, had uttered other law than the mere shout of soldierly command. And he, too, amidst poor, wild, outcast men, had found occasion for deeds of charity such as would not ill have graced the Brethren of the Hospital. His spirit was in sympathy with much of what the canvas showed upon their manly features. Yet, was it not beguiled of that strong tedium, foretaste of time's expansion into eternity, which makes each moment infinite when our waiting mood is not of listlessness, but of intensity.

At last she came. In grander and more touching royalty than even that of sweet and stately maidenhood. Either hand held the fairy fingers of a little daughter, and before her ran a bold and handsome boy.

"See, children! Here's dear uncle Ned."

With that she dropped the tiny soft fingers in her own, and seized the sinewy sun-burnt hands of the brave Indian officer.

So sisterly the light was, which beamed welcome, full and strong, upon him from her kind eyes, that they seemed open windows whence all the dear familiar faces smiled on his return—Robert's and Lucy's, Lady Cransdale's and dear old Phil's, as well.

"Uncle Ned, mamma! Kind uncle Ned, so good to the wild people; and who built them villages?" Such was the question of her eldest daughter, Catherine.

But Reginald, the eldest-born, cried—

"What! our brave uncle Ned, who killed the wicked robber that chopped the children's hands off? Hooray! mamma."

"Constance," said Lady Royston, "what uncles do you pray 'God bless' at night, dear child?"

"Why, uncle Phil and uncle Ned, of course, mamma."

"You hear, Ned, I have kept my word, and not forgotten that I have two brothers."

Not one word came. He only pressed her taper hands; but let them loose at last, and stooped to kiss the children.

"Mother," asked Reggy, as if "mamma" were womanish, "how soon shall I have a big beard, like his?"

But little Constance said—

"It's not so very like the ugly giant's in my picture-book."

Then their pent-up feeling found issue in kindly laughter at the little maid's left-handed compliment. She was in his lap, however, and Reggy at his knee, and even Catherine, more shy in elder childhood, standing with one arm on the back of the great easy-chair in which he sat, when presently Lord Royston came in, to wonder who might be the stranger treated so familiarly. The chorus of childish trebles solved the momentary enigma.

"Here's uncle Ned, papa—the uncle we have never seen—from India!"

"Ned Locksley, Royston," said their mother. "Don't you recognise him?"

Her husband gave him hearty greeting. His was not among those smaller souls which nurse a grudge against the loser of the priceless prize which they themselves have won. And if an imperceptible confusion troubled Ned's acceptance of his cordiality, that was because the younger man was strong enough of heart not easily to pardon unforgotten faults within himself. This slight disturbance was but for an instant. Lord of Rookenham and kinsman of Cransdale, before his marriage with the lovely daughter of its house, Lord Royston had no scanty share in the old associations springing up, faster than even winged words could follow, in conversation fraught with memories, between his wife and Ned. No need of effort, therefore, to keep off that awkwardness which checks the flow of old remembered household talk, by times, when mates of childhood and of early youth meet in the unaccustomed presence of those with whom their later years have mated closer still. The charm of that first hour's intercourse was perfect and unbroken; sudden and unexpected to a marvel, yet unrestrained and easy with the accustomed ease of home.

"Indeed, you are at home, Ned, if Con's privilege may be mine, to give old Cransdale names again. Let me send for your things at once. The broken shaft will take some days to mend, I hear; and there is even talk of turning over passengers and mails to the next boat from Gibraltar."

"And that's the boat by which his cousin comes, if he should come at all," cried Lady Royston. "His dropping from the clouds among us after this sort, had driven that out of my mind entirely."

Then followed explanations. Keane Burkitt, it appeared, had written word that they need not be startled should the next packet from Southampton bring himself to Malta. Besides certain matters of importance to the finance of Rookenham, there were political matters touching my lord's free and independent borough of Cawsley, on which he should be glad to confer personally with my lord, a general election being now most certainly at hand. Moreover, he had been much worked of late; and even Mrs. Burkitt was anxious for him to take the sea trip, though it would part them for a month or two.

"Of course you'll stay for him then, and return together. Are they expecting you at home?"

"How should they be? I came away at eight and forty hours' notice, and the mail's on board the boat which brought me."

"You may write to-morrow by the Sicilian steamer *viâ* Marseilles, I think."

"No! I am almost superstitious on the cup and lip doctrine. Joy breaks no hearts, however it bursts in on them; but disappointment sickens. If you write home by the Sicilian, pray, say nothing of my being half way there."

Then there was Max Gervinus to consider; but on his case the Roystons would suffer no debate.

The official, despatched in quest of Ned's goods from hotel, custom-house, and steamer, was bearer of a note, which took upon themselves the blame of Ned's desertion for these last few hours, and summoned Max with peremptory politeness to become himself at once an inmate of the Palazzo.

"There's only one thing I regret, Ned, on such a happy day as brings you," Lady Royston said.

"Which is?"

"That there is a grand reception here to-night, a dinner, a dance, and I don't know what. All Valetta, besides the garrison. We are not our own, alas! and can't be yours from five o'clock into the smaller hours of night."

Well, it was rather provoking; but there was strange compensation in store for him. After the state-dinner, Ned and Max Gervinus retired to the lofty balcony of their adjoining rooms upstairs. The view was far and wide over the sea, whose waves had now begun to dance instead of dashing, brightening their angry amethystic purple into more limpid hues of sapphire. No speck of cloud remained upon the vault of heaven. None in the west, where the great golden glory was ablaze, although the last rim of the bright orb was sinking. None in the east, where yet the white sails of feluccas glowed with the far refraction of prismatic splendours. But, looking northwards, Ned presently exclaimed—

"Yes, Max! there is one after all. See, how filmy white, yet flushed with filmy pink, and cooled with even filmier shades of blue! Oh, what a lovely cloud, out yonder!"

"Wonder-fine!" Max answered; "but it is too sharp and regular to be a cloud mass. See what a perfect cone. Ah! I have it now, that is the snowy peak of Etna, pink with even-shine."

"Well, I believe you're right, Max."

He went in to fetch his telescope, and having found the focus, gazed long and patiently. Presently he said:

"I see a smoke, like the puff of far-off artillery. Now it rolls out thicker and darker. The wind in

Sicily must be blowing our way this evening; for the smoke hangs towards us like a pall, and has put out my bright cloud altogether."

Then all the sky fell dark, though not with grimy darkness. The sudden southern night had left the heavens blue-black, and the studded diamonds of the stars began to flame and twinkle. By the time they went down into the state rooms again, her ladyship's reception was well crowded; and, in one large saloon, the dancers were keeping joyous time to the strains of a full orchestra. Here and there, among the men in uniform, Ned was greeted by old acquaintances, who had served in Queen's regiments in India. But he knew no lady. The hostess found a moment to ask him if he would not dance, as she would introduce him to Maltese signorina or English girl, as he might fancy. He declined her offer. But Max, with all his scientific gravity was too much of a Teuton to remain indifferent to the, waltz-music. Lady Royston soon made him happy with an accomplished partner. Ned stood more than ever alone. By-and-by, a lady of somewhat more than middle-age came and sat down by an open window near him. Off her winsome countenance his eyes refused to wander when once they had lighted on it. When their fixed gaze attracted hers, she gave no token of any recognition; but something in her look put an end at once to all Ned's hesitation. He stepped forward, held out his hand, and said:

"Surely I cannot be deceived in you. It seems but yesterday since you and your good husband were so kind to me at Chatterham. I fear, dear Mrs. Grant, you have forgotten your former 'griff,' Ned Locksley."

"Not when the voice had spoken half a sentence," she exclaimed, with look and tone and gesture of most friendly reminiscence. "And now I see the old play on the features, and am more glad to see it, Mr. Locksley, than I can easily express."

"And how is the Captain?"

"Major—as I know you will be glad to hear—quite well, I thank you; and will be as much delighted at this meeting as myself."

"Still with the old corps?"

"No:—I am almost sorry to say. For the regiment had become a home to homeless folks like us. But, with our small income, a permanent and better paid appointment such as he holds here, was not to be refused, you know."

"And little Amy?"

"Ah! you would not know *her*. She is not gigantic, yet you would hardly call her little Amy now. But here she is, upon her father's arm."

Yes! There she was! Not short, nor yet of any disproportioned height: as winsome, and even prettier, than ever her mother had been. Of womanly carriage; but of girlish grace. Coy, but lively; with glance of mingled tenderness and mirth; with bright complexion, and features perfectly refined framed in undiminished wealth of the fair golden hair.

Ned was, in peace, a grave enough magistrate, and a soldier grim enough in war; a man who ruled and led successfully, by virtue, of no mean might of self-control. He was no fantastic youth, by this time, with dreamy mind, half awe-stricken, and half cajoled, by the first dawn of passion: yet it befell him that, at this first sight of Amy Grant's unremembered and unfamiliar beauty, he felt his heart kneel down at once to own its sweet dominion.

Sudden as this emotion was, it was so calm as to appear, even to his inmost self, deliberate. Neither his manner, nor his voice, nor yet his look was troubled. He greeted her father partly with the old deference of the recruit for the veteran, partly with the new sense of comradeship, grown of experience, in the same manly school of war.

Amy, at her mother's bidding, gave him her soft hand, as if in old acquaintance, and, little by little, began to gather her childish recollections of him.

They were confused. But a broken-nosed Indian doll, and some name—was it of a "Lady Constance?"—were inextricably bound up with them. Ah! Ned was not going to startle her with his exultation at his suddenly revived reminiscence of their last parting. Yet, as the sheen of her golden hair shifted with the sway of her graceful head, he almost marvelled not to detect the place whence she had shorn the ringlets for him. The frown which knit severity on his bronzed forehead, came of the effort to recall where the too-long neglected treasure might lie hid in his possession.

So completely did the effort absorb his mind, that when the frown relaxed, in the radiance of solution, he was quite surprised to find that Amy Grant was gone, to dance the next quadrille with Max, whom Lady Royston had introduced to her.

The major-domo of their Excellencies was a very good-natured man; but he did think it somewhat unreasonable that, in those smaller hours of night, and when the household were worn out with the fatigues of the great entertainment, this unexpected guest should insist upon his finding two stout lads to carry from the basement-story to his own apartment, up the lofty palace stairs, a ponderous hide-bound trunk, which he had expressly said, need not be moved until it went on board the steam-packet. But the lads forgave him; for, in his generous satisfaction, he forced a dollar into the hand of either, whilst yet their fingers were crooked upon the knotted cords.

He bolted the door on them as they went out, unlocked the trunk, pounced on a little writing-case, and, opening it, tossed its contents out on the bed, to get at the spring of its so-called "secret drawer." He actually shut his eyes on touching it, with nervous fear, lest, after all, proof should jump out of memory's having played him false.

But there the silken coil lay glittering, on a handful of dull brown moss, a few dried rose-leaves scenting it.

It was the most natural thing in the world that, years ago, he should have laid them there together; but to-night it seemed a marvel of delicious omen to find this emblem of a love which might bud unforbidden, cushioned on the memorial of a love to master which had been among the foremost duties of his early youth.

Strange and sweet enchantment, which brought him face to face again with Amy Grant, under the sisterly smile of Constance Cranleigh. Magical compensation! He lay awake, much pondering how soon after the sun was up the jewellers in the Strada dei Orefici would take down their shutters. It must be a locket of the purest crystal, lest the gleam should anywhere be dulled: the plain rim would serve to show how poor a burnish art can put on mere metallic gold.

Unaccountable, perhaps, all this; perhaps unwise. But, once before, I ventured to set down that observation has not shown me what advance men make beyond the wisdom of their generous boyhood, in matters such as these.

At breakfast the next morning Lady Royston said:

"I was so glad, Ned, that you chanced on old acquaintances. I felt less compunction, though not less regret, at leaving you to your own devices all the evening."

"It was the second pleasing wonder of the day," he answered. "I had no notion this time yesterday, outside the harbour, that I should light on you, or on the Grants. You have no notion how kind they were to me when I was a raw recruit at Chatterham."

"I can imagine it. The Major's a thoroughly good-hearted man. His wife is charming. There's no one here in Malta that I like half as well. Amy must have been a child when you were at Chatterham. She is a very nice girl, too."

"A very nice girl," indeed! It was the first falling off that Ned had yet remarked in Lady Royston. She *used* to have exquisite taste and singular felicity of expression.

"I shall ask them all here to dinner, of course."

She had kept her good sense, at least, if her good taste had weakened.

"But not till to-morrow. We must have you one whole evening to ourselves."

Good patience! Had Lady Royston no notion how many minutes make four-and-twenty hours? Not till to-morrow! Was it so certain then that even her good sense was unimpaired. Happily, morning calls, if not often made in the Trans-Nerbuddah, are not abhorrent from the usages of British garrison towns in the Mediterranean. Consolatory thought, whose consolations he lost but little time in seeking to realize. He had no reason to doubt, when he did so, that Mrs. Grant was truly glad to see him; but glad as he was to see her, he would have been gladder not to see her alone. The Major's absence at his office, though to be regretted, might be borne. But that the Grants should know their next-door neighbours, and that their next-door neighbours should have a garden, were things intolerable. What business have people with gardens in Malta, where the soil for the flower-beds must be brought over in speronares all the way from Sicily? Had the garden indeed been at the Grants' own house, one might have suggested a passion for cactus and other prickly beauties of the rocky Maltese flora as a good and sufficient reason for an immediate adjournment thither; but at the next-door neighbours—whom one doesn't happen to know!

How lengthy, deliberate, and minute were his inquiries, not only for the Andersons, but for every soul of the old Chatterham society. His memory seemed to have acquired a sudden faculty for recalling all manner of obsolete names. Mrs. Grant was driven to declare that though her acquaintance with the Major's brother officers at Chatterham was large, it had necessary limits. When the excuse of questioning was at last exhausted, he turned to narrative; and being no setter-forth of self-done deeds, which indeed would have interested his good-natured auditor, he proceeded to ransack his brains for anecdotes, however trivial, of any personages out in India whose most casual acquaintance he could contrive to fasten on her. With all her good-nature, Mrs. Grant began to think him prosy, and the protraction of his call unreasonable; but her woman's wit was quick enough to explain all, and to make allowance for it, when she saw what change came over him, as, at last, the door opened gently, and Amy, with a faldette over her head, came in.

A sallow skin and dark black eyes are generally what that variety of the mantilla shadows under its black silk folds; but when from out their gloom such radiance and such freshness brighten as those of Amy Grant, the unusual contrast has its charms.

"Good morning, Am——I beg a thousand pardons, Miss Grant; but I was thinking of the time when you laughed at me for not knowing the difference between a Spanish mantilla and a Maltese faldette. I have not forgotten it since, I can assure you."

"Indeed!"

"What a wonderful box of dolls that was, Miss Grant. What have you done with them?"

"I gave them to some little cousins, two or three years ago now."

"Well, I hope they did not break their noses, as the rude schoolboys did."

"Which rude schoolboys?"

"Those young ruffians who tied knots in your beautif—in your hair," said Ned, with the absurdest vehemence.

Mrs. Grant could not but smile. Amy, who was indeed "a very nice girl," as Lady Royston had said, and who was free from any undue consciousness of her own attractions, began, nevertheless, to blush rosy red.

Sparks of association run quick in the tinder of memory, and are very luminous besides. His reminiscences of the tangles in her hair began to disentangle some reminiscences of hers. When the least self-conscious of young ladies feels that honest manly eyes are looking no disparagement upon her, when she hears how hard it is for the honest manly voice to keep itself from calling her by her own Christian name; it is a little embarrassing to remember, on a sudden, that, of her own accord, she had once thrust a cluster of her golden curls into the honest manly hand. Even the undoubted fact that it was some nine years or more will not dispel the blush, though it may justify the reckless act of childish generosity.

Happily for her confusion the Major intervened; then lunch, with bitter beer, and so much Chatterham talk again, that even Ned could not resent poor Mrs. Grant's withdrawal from its repetition, though hers determined Amy's.

To-morrow was certainly still very far off, but not quite so distant now as when her ladyship had spoken of it in the morning. He went lionising Max Gervinus about the forts and harbours till late afternoon. Then, an evening spent in company with such people as the Roystons, was certainly no grievous infliction, the less so that they were truly alone, and at their ease, his lordship's secretary having taken Max off to an opera. Without any such dire necessity for stringing questions against time, as had been on him in the forenoon, Ned had plenty to ask and answer.

Phil was still in the Guards, but much less extravagant, and had acquired a taste for fat cattle, which promised well for future landlordism at Cransdale. He always attended the Baker-street show at Christmas. The Maude Cassilis affair had ended long ago to everybody's satisfaction, she having married a gouty marquess. Katey Kilmore, too, had married a clergyman—she was a pattern of grave parochial matrons now. Phil's latest indications had been towards Lady Rosa Barrington. The Buffer, by the way, had lost his father as well as his elder brother, an old bachelor, and so come in to the Bamford title. Thus, Rosa was "her ladyship." Mamma thought her a little too saucy, perhaps, but she had improved even on that score, and was such a bright good-natured girl that if Master Phil and she were to grow serious, the banns would not be forbidden. Hebblethwaite minor was in the heavy dragoons; was six feet high, and rode over fifteen stone. Young Mapes, of Maperley, the squire's son, had turned out much cleverer than any of them had given him credit for, and was doing well at the Chancery Bar. Yes, old Mrs. White was still alive at Rookenham, and in nominal possession of the keys, but her asthma would hardly let her mount the first flight of stairs, so that Martha, who was head housemaid formerly, was a sort of coadjutor and successor-designate. Police-Constable Hutchins had risen to be chief-inspector under the captain superintendent of the county police. He was married, and had divers children. Ah, poor Benjy! he was drowned after all, in a pool not far from the Pixie's pillar. Rizpah's desolation had been at first most lamentable, but as the poor lad's reason had grown dimmer, if any thing, it was really merciful that he had not grown up to helpless manhood on her hands.

Then Lady Royston turned examiner, and Ned must needs, with what modest reserve he might, disclose to her wherein old aspirations after action on the great Eastern field had been fulfilled or frustrated.

That was a charmingly spent evening, after all. When Max and the Secretary came in for a late cup of coffee, the stay-at-homes opined that it must have been a very short opera.

A choice not wisely made is often not unwise in itself. Happy the man to whom so great and undeserved a grace is given. When judgment may rest content where fancy has been toiled, large indeed is the debt that hearts owe to heaven. Hardly shall they write it in sufficient figures upon their tablet of obligations.

Not that Ned's judgment had put off, next day, the tinted spectacles of fancy, nor bound on again the bandage which shuts all illusion out; nor yet that his decisions on points raised for consideration were as deliberate and as impartial as if he sat in magisterial "cutcherry" among his Bheels.

But even had Lucy Locksley, or some critic of equally keen sight, been scrutinizing Amy Grant, the verdict on her looks and bearing could not have been unfavourable. The tests applied, as if by chance, to both were certainly severe. Though mother of three children, Lady Royston had lost little of the lustre of her beauty. Wife and companion of a man of higher mark in politics than even in society, she had but added loftier dignity to the exquisite grace which always had distinguished her.

It was impossible, as it would have been unfair, to institute comparison between her and the younger girl. Yet excellence of any real kind creates around itself an atmosphere of light, in which all other excellence shows gem-like, whilst every coarser or defective thing is seen for what it is, dulling the ray which falls, or refracting it distorted.

Now, Amy Grant, even side by side with Lady Royston, still seemed attractive, lady-like, and full of graceful animation. She sat at dinner between Ned and Max Gervinus, he having Lady Royston on his other hand. Max had a gift of conversation, possessing not only the erudition of a scientific German, but the German poetic temperament as well. His was good talk, full-bodied, well-flavoured, and of rich hue, as wine of some choice vintage in the fatherland. The party was small and the table oval. There was not that tieing of talk to couples, which, perhaps, under these peculiar circumstances, Ned might not have thought as irksome as do most times the condemned to dinner customs. Both he and Amy had to take their part in the conversation of Max and Lady Royston. When Amy spoke, it was with spirit and intelligence.

Another ordeal remained for her that evening, which Ned himself might better be trusted to watch with jealous keenness. A whole batch of young officers came in, as if her Excellency had held a levée for the Queen.

Brought up among such types of womanhood as his own mother, Lady Cransdale, and her daughter Constance, it was little wonder that Ned, when he first went to Chatterham, should have felt strong distaste for the character of a garrison-belle. The word, though somewhat indefinite, is perhaps sufficiently expressive. Bombay society, and such sparse experiences as occasional visits from his remoter district to more European "stations" had afforded him in India, had certainly done nothing towards lessening the original distaste. Few men would have been quicker to detect a trace of the obnoxious characteristics; none would have been more instantaneously disenchanted by the detection. Major Grant's business brought him in contact with almost every officer in Malta, and chary as he and his wife might be of vulgarizing introductions to their daughter, it was impossible, short of secluding her, to prevent her from having a wide circle of military acquaintances.

Ned watched—without misgiving, it is true, yet with appreciative observation—not only how the lady of his thoughts received her soldier friends, but in what tone and with what carriage they ventured to address her. He exulted, not unpardonably, at perceiving that scarcely did their stately hostess command more genuine deference than his winsome Amy. Here was indeed a token, to the coldest prudence, of her true love-worthiness—a token, doubtless, too, to Ned, that his own choice was meritorious and his intuition deep.

CHAPTER XII.

Keane came. Ned would, of course, return with him. So there were some ten precious days before him, a delay at which his homeward haste no longer fretted, for all his dutiful and tender sonship.

His cousin Keane was just the man to give him sage advice upon a topic which had suddenly acquired new importance in his eyes—the best investment to be made of the fortune left him by the dear old Brigadier. For it was almost a fortune, so long had the accumulation been and so slender the frugal veteran's draughts upon it. Keane was soon put in possession of its existence and amount—soon set reflecting upon the most advantageous use that might be made of it. On one point Ned was positive. He would have no dabbling in the railway share-market, which was just then, or perhaps, more strictly, had been but just before, the Eldorado of adventurous financiers. It was not the risk he feared, so much as the principle he repudiated. Indeed, his notions on the matter had a smack of primitive intolerance. It was not simply that share jobbing was gambling in his estimation, and therefore execrable; but what might be considered its most legitimate gains were in his eyes little else but fraudulent. It was not simply that "rigs," and "plants," and "dodges," rose up from lower jobbing regions, as foul unusual miasmata to taint the atmosphere; but, in his moral chemistry, the purest air of that market was at best "malaria." "Premiums" he looked upon as "loot" or plunder, not won in open war, but treacherous ambuscade; and there was no getting him to understand that "preference shares" were not necessarily the product of some "scoundrelly piece of favouritism."

Lord Royston, indeed, half in fun, took up the cudgels against him, for some open outrageous declaration of the sort made over the city-articles of the English newspapers which the mail had brought to hand. But if confused in argument, Ned was strong in instances drawn from other columns of those same journals, of the demoralizing and ruinous effects of this peculiar form of speculation.

Keane, who had his old command of countenance, took no decided part in this amicable controversy, nor did he betray any personal interest in the debated matter. On the whole, he leaned rather to Ned's side than his lordship's; and, at all events, encouraged the former to speak out his indignation, and to discover how genuine was its warmth even if its light were not so brilliant.

Another day, however, brought "overland" advices from England, of several days' later date; and the newspapers furnished Ned with occasion for a fresh diatribe. The first heavy drop of a financial thunderstorm had fallen thick. It taxed Keane's composure to the utmost, to hear among a list of names, involved in the preliminary catastrophes, that of Walter Sherbrooke, junior, who some years back had parted partnership with that "slow coach, the governor." Ned read it, without emphasis, among a string of others; but it sounded as a knell in Keane's quick ear.

That same afternoon he hurried on, although with admirable tact and skill, the conversation which he had not intended, until after gradual and due preparation, to hold with his lordship concerning the Cawsley borough. Many a step made off perilous ground into Parliament has found footing firm enough to secure recovery of an endangered balance. But the case was hopeless. Lord Royston had but just received the letter which told him that the Solicitor-General was dead; and that the man named to succeed him had not a seat in Parliament. His colleagues hoped he saw no objection to the self-immolation of the sitting member, and the election of the new Crown lawyer. This was a thunder-stroke for Keane.

By-and-by his letters came. Some blunder at the post-office had kept them from him in the morning. Do what he could, his features, when he came down from his room again, would tell of some disturbance. Lady Royston did not seem to notice it as she inquired if all were well at home; but Ned marked something of the effort with which he answered in the affirmative.

He was not, therefore, much surprised at the sorrowful gravity which showed through the composure with which his cousin bore himself as he came, late, for private conversation into his own room.

"What's up, Keane? Nothing wrong at Freshet, unless you took Lady Royston in."

"No, nothing wrong at Freshet," he said.

"Not at Cransdale, then? For heaven's sake don't keep me in suspense, man!"

For Keane did not answer at first, but sat down, looking at him wistfully.

"I am afraid, from what I have heard you say, that you, at least, will think it wrong."

"What on earth do you mean? Are my father and mother well?"

"For all I know, they are. But I am in a sad strait to tell you. I fear to violate a confidence."

Ned folded his arms and looked at him with expectation. It was no use uttering a string of questions at a venture.

"Give me your word of honour that what I may say passes your lips to no man, not even to him whom, personally, it most concerns."

"May I do it, honourably?"

"Should I have asked you, otherwise?" said Keane, in a quiet tone of reproof, which his cousin felt intimately.

"I beg your pardon, and pass you my word."

"Well, then, this railway mania, against which you were speaking with such vehemence, you must know that it has infected all classes of society in England."

Ned stared at him in utter amazement, not having an inkling of what his drift might be.

"Adventurous speculators, whether fradulent or not, are but a fraction of the crowd who elbow their way into the share-list. The most staid and sober of our men of business may be counted in that crowd, with hundreds of higher eminence, and of even more acknowledged worth. When you were planning your schedule of moral proscription you little knew what names must fill it up."

"My dear fellow, forgive me," interrupted Ned, "but what conceivable connexion can there be between all this and any thing wrong at Cransdale?"

"If you must have it in one word," Keane answered, with evident pain, "I fear—indeed I know—my uncle has had some large transactions."

"What, my father?" Ned asked tremulously, shading his eyes with one hand, as if to hide their sudden sadness.

"Yes."

There followed a short silence, then Ned spoke again—

"It seems incredible. No man was ever more generous, none ever less grasping, than my father."

"You do him no more than justice."

"What, then, can have induced him?"

"What you must be the last to blame—a wish to leave a larger inheritance to you. Men are often tempted on the good side of their qualities," quoth Keane, with a sad, moralising smile, full of compassion.

The saying carried conviction. Ned's own experience acknowledged its closeness to the truth. He was much troubled: rose up and went walking to and fro. Presently he sat down again and asked—

"Is that all the bad news, Keane; or is there any thing behind?"

"I have had warning to-day that his transactions have turned out little short of disastrous."

"What, have you heard from him, then?"

"No; but from a man through whose hands all his purchases and sales of shares have passed. Here, you read out his name yourself this morning as among the most involved—Walter Sherbrooke, junior, share and stock broker."

He held the paper across to Ned in confirmation, pointing with his finger to the name.

Then he proceeded to give him, in language not wholly intelligible to the soldier, what yet appeared to be precise, business-like, and legal details of the transactions in which his uncle had engaged himself in a sort of joint responsibility with Walter Sherbrooke.

"It is a sad business. Your poor, dear father will feel it more acutely for your mother's sake and for yours than for his own."

Ned covered his face with both hands now.

"I have not dared to mention it to the Roystons," Keane went on. "I am sure it will cut them to the quick; and still more the Cransdales. Of course, my uncle's integrity will come out spotless."

"I should think so," burst in poor Ned, with a proud indignation.

"But an error in judgment of that sort shakes confidence in a man of business—when he goes out of his way, too, to court the mischief. I cannot say how I regret this rashness on the part of one so prudent as your father."

"Do not talk so, Keane. I would sooner charge a battery or stand a volley at a dozen yards. Can nothing be done to mend matters at once?"

He was up again once more, and pacing to and fro again.

"Nothing is a hard word. Let me see."

He opened a letter and read, with knit brow; then brought out a pencil and made calculations on the back of it. Ned, passing and re-passing, sentry-like, eyed him with growing anxiety.

"Let me see," muttered Keane; "the French mail leaves to-morrow. From Marseilles one could telegraph, and let him know the cheque was on its way. Large as Sherbrooke's deficit is, a much less sum in ready money than the total would clear them yet, he says, with ease. But, in the present state of the money market, and known as he is to have this unfortunate scrip on hand, he cannot find accommodation on any terms nor for any security. Tell me, Ned—it is a bold question I shall put—would you be willing to risk, if necessary, the Brigadier's whole legacy?"

"In what way risk it—in fresh speculations?"

"No; but in a composition such as might clear your father's liability forthwith."

"Risk it for that! I would sink it, every farthing!"

"Well, I said 'risk,' because your father *might* retrieve his loss hereafter. I imagine it is a present desperate pressure that is on him, rather than a stroke which will cripple his resources once for all."

"And if it were such a stroke he would need the money all the more. What's mine is his."

Then flashed upon him once again remembrance

of his boyish saying under the Cransdale cedars, uttered in his own ears but yesterday by the dying Hindoo boy—"What a father owes a son owes." Ned's mind was one that meant its words, and would redeem their pledge without once flinching.

So, when his cousin Keane had again thought out, turned over, and partly made him understand his scheme, it was agreed that Walter Sherbrooke should have authority to draw upon the firm of Burkitt and Goring. But, inasmuch as their large balance at the bankers was much of it trust-money or deposit-money of their numerous and confidential clients, Ned gave his cheque on Messrs. Cox and Co., in whose hands were his whole resources, to his Cousin Keane, to cover every risk the firm might run. One or both of them would take passage by the Marseilles boat to-morrow, to reach as soon as possible the telegraphic wires. But by the morrow Ned had taken a new determination.

With what look should he face his father? Were it consciousness of any fault or folly of his own which troubled it, a few frank words, and a few moments' open gaze, would chase, as they had always chased of old, the momentary mist away. But the sadness of the present murky cloud was strange and new. It hung about his father's deed. How should a son's brow dare to frown, or even smile, such cloud away? Mean souls may think that their own stature gains in height as that of others dwindles. The nobler feel as if themselves grew less at every lowering of the standard whereby they needs must measure what were kindred souls. Making compassionate allowance, where once they paid full reverence, humiliates and pains, and sickens generous hearts. Yet they, themselves, can bear with pain, with sickness, with humiliation. They most dread dooming others to the bearing. What, if the sight of him inflicted either on his father? What, if his very silence should seem to utter a reproach, or even his suspected pity mortify?

Then there was his mother. What if she should feel as he felt? What if she should speak as he must, should he speak at all? Which were the worst, a tacit conspiracy or an open agreement in verdict, against one whom it were almost impious to arraign at bar before them? Subjects empannelled to try sovereigns were surely less disloyal; their procedure less incongruous! This unexpected coming might betray her into outpouring of some confidence, which soon she might wish recalled; or it might weight her burden with the irksomeness of an unnatural constraint. Her wife's heart would find it easy to make a husband's apology to its own self; her mother's heart might shrink from pleading a father's excuses to a son.

He might be sparing her a keener sorrow in keeping from her the unanticipated joy. She knew not, she need never know, how much the weary distances were once diminished between her only son's embrace and her own ever longing arms.

Yes. It were better so. His cousin should have full power to act for him. He should settle, if it might be, with this Sherbrooke, after such sort that Robert Locksley, too, should never know of his son's costly sacrifice. Costly, beyond reckoning of cost. Not for the money's sake. Ten times the sum in gold had seemed a trifle to him, were it not for the lost hopes of which those golden threads of Amy's hair would be to him henceforth the sad if sweet reminder.

There was an end, a second time in life, of such a dear illusion. It was a plainer issue than the first time between love and duty, and he was now too well-accustomed servant of the one to dally out of season with allurements of the other.

It was fantastic torment yesterday to think that the few days which had so bound his heart to her, must needs leave hers unfettered; to-day the vexing thought gave consolation, since no regret of hers would follow him. Such cordials, healthful in their bitterness, will duty mingle in the cup of disappointment for brave lips, which, at her bidding, do not blench to drink.

Had it been otherwise; had he preferred his suit, and had it prospered, there might have been a conflict between a pledged word and the duties of an altered circumstance. Now, there was none. He had no right to sue that she should link her life to that of a poor subaltern, whose only portion was his sword; who yet might need, for all he knew, to stint himself of that sword's meagre wage to meet a father's or a mother's sharp necessity. His first care, therefore, in the morning was to take a pledge of Keane that he would not, of his own act, lose an hour on the way to England; his next, to execute all necessary legal forms to put his cousin in condition to use the uttermost of resources. Should these prove inadequate, Keane insisted that he might be allowed to share in clearing his uncle's affairs from the disasters of Walter Sherbrooke's failure.

"With such a good heart as that speaks, Keane, and your known clear head to guide it, the matter is safest in your hands alone. And they should not be fettered. Consulting me could only hamper your decision. Any attempt to clear my ignorance could but waste time in which your enlightened judgment might be acting. There is no need for me to go with you. I shall return to India. I can go outward with lighter heart than homeward now."

The steamers which went either way would leave that night. Keane's departure, though earlier than his hosts had reckoned on, called for no special explanation beyond the simple notice that his letters had determined it. He and Lord Royston, as good men of business, despatched the Rookenham affairs that afternoon. Ned meanwhile spoke to Lady Royston, openly even in reserve. The man hated subterfuge, and would use none. Trustful himself, he was bold to claim ungrudging trust. It pained him to ask of her a promise that she and her husband would maintain for good and all the silence they had kindly kept upon his presence with them hitherto. Little had he thought how it should help him when he first had asked them to observe it. An unexpected crisis in his life had come. He must not show upon what hinge it turned; that was a secret not his own. He was no weathercock, she might believe, although he veered upon that hinge so suddenly, and once more pointed eastward.

"Your gentle breath turned me that way once, dear Lady Royston. This time it is another wind."

"A chilling one, I fear, dear Ned, since it blows you back from home."

He could not trust himself to say much more, but answered with a wistful pleasantry—

"At any rate, it blows me back to warm work again in India. Will you kindly make excuses for me to the Grants, and say the suddenness of my departure did not allow me to present them, as I should have done, myself."

Max Gervinus was inconsolable when he, too, learnt how strangly soon the cord of so good companionship must snap.

"What must be must; but I dare stay no longer here, my friend, with this most charming lord and lady. I go not without you to England. I travel by Marseilles with your cousin, and thence through Switzerland to Germany once more. Ah, mine heart is heavy, Ned! Saw you not what cloud darkened the pink Etna-snow that first heavenly evening time? Now comes such omen true!"

But when the last good-bye was said on either side that night, and Lady Royston, with her husband, stood upon the farthest rocks of Point

Dragut,—when she had waved her handkerchief the last time seaward, watching the steamer's hulls grow less as they diverged still more and more,—she noted that the homeward-bound went steering into darkness, the outward-bound along the glistening track of moonlight on the sea.

CHAPTER XIII.

The hazardous game that Keane had played was won more easily and thoroughly than he had dared to hope. His ingenuity had not been taxed for details. He had but lessened the proportions of the true disaster, putting his uncle's name in substitution for his own. The story thus seemed genuine by many tokens. The risk had been, not in the bold suggestion that such a man as Ned should venture all to save the credit of a father's name, but in endeavouring to get hold himself upon the sum adventured. Having first put a seal of secrecy upon his cousin's lips, he doubted not, though they should go home together, that he himself must act for him in some early stage of the affair. His own craft and quickness could be trusted to seize on even a moment's opportunity.

Ned's resolve spared him even that critical moment.

He had no foolish hope of retrieving himself at home. The mere conception of the new misdeed proved that as he had been always utterly selfish, he was not now for the first time fraudulent. The Sherbrooke crash not only broke his wealth, but, he well knew, must also break his character. Some things might be glozed over, but enough must come to light to ruin a man whose whole resources lay in the confidence of others. On a complete review of circumstances, he had determined to accept his defeat as total on the old position. That must be shifted. He would not return to Freshet. But go where he might, he was not the man to endure the thought of facing destitution or even a contented inactivity in straitened means. Sophy's patrimony was secured to her own use and disposal. Even should she feel inclined to share it with him, it was not available as capital, and could furnish no basis for future operations. But this money of his cousin's, available at once, would be the very thing he wanted. How get leave to finger it? No pretext of profitable speculation would serve the turn. Ned had no greed of gold, strange as it seemed, though, for some reason unexpressed, he wished to place his money to the best secure advantage.

Then came the sudden evil inspiration. Half amused at Ned's philippics against the share jobbers, some of the sharp indignant words had stung him through his moral hide. There was a smack of diabolic humour in pricking his censorious cousin with the goad of self-reproach for having thus condemned his father among the men he scorned.

The jest might be severely practical, but it would clear itself in time without much hurt to father or to son.

As for the money, Ned could better afford to lose than he to want it. It was a windfall, come by chance, and gone without much serious damage to the son of one so well-to-do as Robert Locksley. Who knew but what some day, if restitution should seem to be a luxury, he might himself indulge in it, and repay Ned with interest this sort of secretly-forced loan?

When the dullest man consents to hold a devil's brief against his conscience, he soon becomes a clever special pleader in the case. But Keane Burkitt was a man by no means dull.

Meanwhile there was an uneasiness concerning

him at Freshet from the first intimation had there of the calamities of Walter Sherbrooke. Cautiously as Keane had veiled that connexion from public notice, its existence had not remained a perfect secret, if its extent was unsuspected still. When speculations prospered, Keane never made an insolent display. His ambition aimed higher and was biding its time. Yet he had evident success enough, on whatever field, to kindle jealousy, and so to set Argus eyes a-watch. Such began to wink with suggestion, not with sleep, when his trip to Malta was seen to coincide so nearly with stormy days in Capel-court. Winkers soon came to mutter, mutterers to chatter. Preliminary meetings of creditors *in re* Sherbrooke, junior, began to gather in town. Intelligence oozed out thence that "the name of a principal partner in a highly confidential firm of solicitors in a well-known watering place, upon the Blankshire coast, was assuming prominence in the insolvent's affairs." All Freshet read this in the London papers before the local journals thought it safe to reproduce the paragraph within snap of the firm's formidable teeth. Old Mr. Goring went up to town. There was not much, perhaps, in that. In his absence, however, a significant circumstance occurred. A letter came to the office—so a newly indentured clerk was green enough to babble—bearing Lord Royston's signature and the Malta postmark. It was evident that Mr. Burkitt had left that island if ever he had reached it. This first frightened Sophy. Till then she had made up her mind that Keane's long silence came of some post-office accident alone. When comments on the matter reached her ear, her heart misgave her somewhat. But her sister Fanny met these misgivings with quick indignation. She was not one to set a man down all unworthy because of his unworthy treatment of herself. She had taken down the image from its once high stand without having had Sophy's forced occasions to study all its disproportions, to trace the cracks which seamed its marble, and to know the real coarseness of its grain throughout. Besides, she was most anxious that the weakness of his wife's surmises should not do for his mother the work of the world's injustice. Why should her widowed heart be troubled with apprehensions which must turn out unfounded or exaggerated? But on Mr. Goring's return from London they proved to be too well founded, and even exaggeration seemed excusable when the barest truth turned out to be so very serious. That is, so far as money losses were involved. The slippery nature of the share dealing tricks was not yet evident. Keane's dishonesty had all along been strangely inconsistent. Many men, who did as he did, divide their lives, and whether from mere happy inconsistency or from calculated hypocrisy, are rogues in counting-houses or chambers, honest men enough in their more private dealings. Now he had made a further subdivision of his life, not one which can be counted likely to have endured under pressure of extreme temptation, but of which the separating line had not yet been transgressed when all his private ventures shivered in Walter Sherbrooke's ruin. Having grasped, and griped, and cheated in the share-market, he had yet betrayed no client's interest in his capacity as confidential solicitor. At least Mr. Goring could discover nothing irregular, nothing suspicious, no disorder, no defalcation, in any matter touching the business of the firm. This to him was, of course, an infinite relief. He was surprised to find how little it seemed so to his partner's wife.

But the luxurious ease in which she had lived hitherto had thoroughly possessed her affections. A stranger to insatiable aspirations, she had yet never been indifferent to the position which her qualities as mistress of a wealthy house had secured for her in the society of their little seaport town. She was one of those mothers, moreover, whose temper is lavish of indulgence to the expensive caprices of her children. And when it was proved to hèr that house and horses, delicate fare, fine dress, and costly toys, were swept off in the current of her husband's calamity, she almost forgot her personal anxieties about him, and seemed to throw up her hands as one who will sink with wailing but without a struggle in the flood.

"Her weakness is contemptible, my dear;" would Mr. Goring say to his own matter-of-fact old wife; "she sobs and sobs lace pocket-handkerchiefs with tears, and cries, 'O cruel, cruel, Keane!' whenever I come to definite proposals. I want authority from some one to rout out and sort up what papers he has left at his own house, now that I have almost done with those at the office."

"Why not try Mrs. Burkitt, senior?" she would answer; "there's starch in her that no stream of tears will ever wash out, I guess."

Mrs. Goring, apparently, took a severe view of that lady's character. Passages in their former life might once have justified it.

"Why, Miss Davenant has threatened me with I

don't know what, if I worry his mother about him. I am sure I don't know what to do."

"Make Miss Davenant herself take her silly sister in hand. She has common sense enough for both. You should know that by this time."

"A very good suggestion, my dear," said Mr. Goring, and forthwith acted on it.

Nothing could have been better thought of. Sophy, not without some foolish and unjust reproaches of her sister for needless or hurried interference, was at last persuaded to let her and her husband's partner do as they thought fit. Still no traces of any but heavy pecuniary embarrassments revealed themselves to the search of the latter. Fanny was in exultation, not only because the more malignant rumours against the man whom once she had thought not unworthy of her heart were likely to prove mere slanders, but because a light began to dawn upon the hope of a deliverance from his difficulties.

"The only thing which staggers me, Miss Davenant, is his protracted silence."

"I only see in it a proof," she answered, "that he is more sensitive than some have thought him;" and this interpretation she urged upon her aunt, the quarter whence she looked for his possible rescue.

She still had no precise knowledge of that old lady's resources, none whatever of her testamentary dispositions. But she was aware of her strong partiality to Keane, and of the substantial proofs of it afforded by her liberality upon his marriage. All might yet be well, and much be spared, even of the fantastic humiliations, which her sister dreaded, if it should only prove that Aunt Davenant had will and power to make for him a large and honourable composition.

Something smote that little old lady at the eagerness of Fanny's pleading.

"My dear niece, I like openness. Why did not Sophy come herself to me? She knows, much better than you can, my feeling for her husband, to say nothing of my treatment of herself, which might have given you sometimes some excuse for jealousy."

"You were always the kindest of aunts to me," said Fanny.

Sincerely meant in one way, the answer, in another, was evasive. Fanny, in fact, had acted without consulting her sister, who might have conceived unmeasured hopes, and suffered, should the notion prove unfruitful, unmeasured disappointment.

"I am not sure of that, my dear; but, if so, to her I have been kinder than kindest. I suppose she sent you to me."

To this she made no answer, so the old lady put the question more explicitly—

"Did Sophy send you here, my dear, or not?"

"No, she did not; and, I dare say, feels that from herself an application such as this would look like an encroachment upon one who has been so generous."

The elder woman felt that only fine hearts find apologies of this kind readily. She was the more troubled as she asked again—

"Is it for your sister's sake, then, that you come to me, my dear?"

Fanny would not prevaricate, so held her peace again.

Her aunt had more than once seen Sophy since the extent of Keane's losses had been, with some certainty, surmised. She had been struck and pained by his wife's selfish querulousness and by her apparent scantiness of thought for him. Her rising indignation quickened apprehension in her mind of what significance might lie in Fanny's different concern and forethought. Presently she said—

"How far do you think, my dear, that I have power to help him?"

That she could not say, save in a loose conjecture. But her aunt's previous liberality had shown that her resources were far greater than had been usually supposed; she knew the kindness of her heart, and so had ventured to conceive a hope that even at a sacrifice—

"Sacrifice is a fine thing to *recommend*," Miss Davenant interrupted, drily; "another guess to practise."

"True; but the satisfaction must be grand and deep."

"If you mean that, Fanny, prove it."

In a few, quiet, business-like sentences she told her niece what division of her property she had made by will, and how she had anticipated, in favour of the Burkitts on their marriage, by far the greater part of the larger provision she had made for Sophy.

"If my money can right matters, my dear, it can only do so at your own expense, you see. I fear I have done you injustice enough already. Of my own accord I will do you no more. If the sacrifice is made, you make it.

Without an instant's deliberation, Fanny rose,

crossed over to the arm-chair in which her aunt was sitting, lifted the Persian cat with becoming respect out of her lap, knelt down, folded her taper waist with both arms most lovingly, kissed her upon either withered cheek, and said—

"God bless you, auntie. May I tell Mr. Goring, then, to take the necessary steps at once with Mr. Sherbrooke's creditors?"

Tears glistened in the old lady's bright, little eyes.

"Fanny, dear, you have a great heart; but a great fear troubles me that I have wronged it. God knows the thought was far from me. If you will answer me one question that may pain you, it *might* give me an infinite relief, selfish as it may be to say so."

"Speak your mind out, dear auntie."

"Openly, then, my dear good niece, and honestly: was there ever any thing, any engagement, understanding—you know what I mean—between yourself and Keane before he married Sophy?"

"Nothing more, dear aunt," she said, "than this—which I found again when searching his own private desk with Mr. Goring yesterday."

It was her own small glove, whose fellow had

gone eddying upon the swirl of Thames at Twickenham.

"And this is your revenge! Now, God requite you for it, Fanny."

It may be that He had already. He had spared her, at least, the cruel chill by inches which must creep upon the warmest heart if laid a life-long beside another such as Keane's. That very day, on her return from Lanercost, she found poor Sophy shivering over the selfish coldness of a letter from New York, in which her husband wrote that he had thought it best to try to push his way there without incumbrance either of wife or child.

CHAPTER XIV.

TIME had sufficed during Ned's short absence from India for the gathering of new war clouds over a fresh field of strife. British soldiers of a younger generation were to try conclusions with a foe of name and face familiar to their elders. Trouble was rife again with the Mahrattas; the rock of Gwalior seemed to attract the thunderstorm. Locksley's Horse, as they were now called for short, had been withdrawn from Scinde to join the army assembling under Gough's command. Thither, immediately on his return, their leader hurried, glad of such exciting action as might divert his thoughts from the sad interruption of his homeward voyage.

His coming caused a jubilee among the swarthy troopers. O'Brien, indeed, had shown them at

Meeanee in what sort he was worthy to lead such men as they; but time had been denied him to conciliate in any large degree the confident and passionate attachment which bound them to Ned Locksley.

Great was, especially, the exultation of the Bheel. He had predicted the sure return of his own sahib before swords should be crossed again. No arguments of the One-eyed, drawn from geographical considerations, had moved him from that firm persuasion. The Kattiwaree, therefore, and his equipments were in such condition that one might have thought his master had given orders but the day before to saddle him for the march. Bikhu could not resist such reference to the fulfilment of his own anticipations as caused the worthy jemadar to shake his head and mutter against the magic sources of the misbeliever's information. Nusreddeen and Bikhu met, however, upon a common ground of congratulation, not only on the sahib's own arrival, but on the fact that in his company was come the great shikaree, Sergeant-Major Wilmot. Locksley had found him in Bombay, returned to regimental duty, and arrived at the superior non-commissioned rank.

The gallant Europeans were not for service in

the threatening campaign; and, irregular as the proceeding was, Ned, an absentee of whom his colonel and his corps were proud, obtained leave for his Cransdale follower to make it with his old friends of the Trans-Nerbuddah.

The camp itself was honoured, not to say perplexed—as readers know, who keep in memory the features of that short decisive warfare—by the presence of no less a personage than the Governor-General. His suite and staff commingled with the following of the General in command, increased the usual difficulty of ascertaining, suddenly, on what company a new arrival might have chanced. Indeed, Ned's first and second days in camp enlightened him but little on that head, being engrossed with the business of resuming his own small command. O'Brien, known to the General-in-Chief, his fellow countryman, was easily consoled for the transfer by an appointment upon his personal staff.

It was not till the third evening, that Ned, at home again with all the details of the condition of his corps, and ready, as in old Scindian times, for any service at a moment's notice, betook himself for a stroll of social exploration through the lines. Here and there a friendly hand met his, and words of soldierly welcome from an old comrade cheered him. But, as he neared the Governor-General's quarters, he felt a grasp upon his elbow from behind.

"Locksley, of Locksley's Horse, if I mistake not?"

The voice brought but a dim remembrance; and the features, ill discerned in the growing dusk, brought little else.

"Just so. But, I beg pardon. In fact, I fear you have the advantage of me."

"Pray don't mention it; but do me the favour to step this way with me. There is a lady here, whom you may recognise, and who is, herself, most anxious to set eyes on you."

A little bungalow stood some fifty paces to the rear of the rearmost line of tents: thither Ned's unknown acquaintance piloted him. At a table, in the room which opened into the verandah, sat a lady, writing by the light of a lamp, already lit.

"Here, my lady," quoth the officer, "I have obeyed your royal behests, and captured Mr. Locksley."

"Miss Florence Barrington!" cried Ned, as she rose to greet him.

"As was," answered the officer. "Since gazetted, 'Lady Sangster.'"

"Then, you had not heard of our marriage?" asked Florence, with his hand in hers.

"Certainly not," interrupted her husband, "or he would have hanged himself, which, I suppose, that I must do, now that he has turned up again. You don't happen to have a forage rope about you, Mr. Locksley? There's a nice tree with a crooked branch outside."

Ned stared, as well as he might. Florence only laughed, and shook her forefinger, with menace, at her husband, as she used to do at her vivacious cousin.

"Yes, that was the way you shook your finger at poor dear honest Rosy, when she let your cat out of the bag. She told me, Mr. Locksley, not to flatter myself too much on Florence's acceptance of my suit, for she only took *me*, because you had neglected to take *her*."

"For shame, Willie! How can you? You knew his old way, Mr. Locksley, and can hear he's not altered for the better."

"Ah, well! I'm a blighted being. Never mind, your ladyship, the campaign may make a widow."

Wherewith he applied a handkerchief to his eyes, so comically, that spite of the too sad probability with which he jested, his wife and visitor burst out into laughter.

"It is really too bad of you!" cried the former,

when they begun to recover breath; but Willie, or rather, Sir William, being incorrigible, only bowed, and blew a kiss to her. Ned now found opportunity to offer his double congratulations. Of Sangster's promotion he had been before aware, but had not heard of the marriage, at which he could heartily rejoice.

"I cannot conceive what made me hesitate to recognise you, when the voice, too, sounded so familiarly. But it was very dusky, and you came on me from behind, you know. I had no notion you were attached to Sir Hugh Gough's army."

"No more I aint. I came, promiscuous, with the Governor-General. Flo. heard, however, that Lady Gough was with her husband, and nothing would induce her to stay behind. Seen 'general orders' to-night, eh?"

"No, I haven't. Any thing particular?"

"Only that we, with Gough, march upon Maharajpore to-morrow; Grey's wing on Punniar. Khajee Wallah and the Maharanee don't seem to see things Lord Ellenborough's way."

"Will the Mahrattas fight?"

"Like mischief. I am told they are intrenching themselves across the Kohuree River."

"I was in hopes," said Lady Sangster, "that

matters might have gone off in negotiation. Many chiefs have sent their vakeels into camp, you know."

"To throw dust in his lordship's eyes," her husband answered.

"Well, it don't take much of a scuffle to raise dust in this camp," said Ned. "I wish it would rain before the march, for Lady Sangster's sake. You have no notion what a cloud an Indian army tramps in."

"Too good luck to rain," replied Sir William; "though I dare say it's snowing fast at home."

"Where at home, dear?"

"At home in England, to be sure; have you forgotten it is Christmas time?"

Into what memories did that one word beguile them. Forgetful of the weary march before them —forgetful of the grim encounter to which the march would lead—forgetful almost, bride and bridegroom, of their own exclusive new-found happiness—forgetful almost, solitary disappointed heart, of all its troubles, there they sat far on into the soft, warm, Indian night, recalling earliest scenes, thoughts, feelings, and associations from the bright hearths whose blazing kindled once more out of remembered Christmas hours at home.

And yet Ned's heart would ache, less from regret than sharp anxiety.

What if his own eyes caught no Christmas cheer from camp-fires glaring upon dusky heathen forms. At least, the brightness of that hearth at home by which he might not sit, would not be darkened by the fall of even shadowy dishonour. For that his manly heart was well contented to forego even the homeless happiness, asking no home, which his friend Florence and her soldier husband found upon the restless march, each in the other's dear companionship.

But on him a sickening impatience lay to know that it was truly so; to hear from Keane that his dear father's name was clear; thus to be certified that his heartwhole sacrifice, at least, was timely. A mail reached the camp the very night they pitched it by the stream which parted the hostile forces.

No sadder token was needed of the change in poor Ned's life than just the shiver, wherewith he recognised his own dear mother's hand writing upon the solitary letter brought him.

His mother's hand; not Keane's!

To think that this should be a cruel disappointment.

Strong soldier as he was, his fingers trembled almost too much to break the seal. Then with one hasty notice of the date, the eye went glancing down the pages, fearing alike to catch or not to catch some word significant of shame or sorrow. Presently Keane's name arrests it; Keane's, and in close contact, Sherbrooke's! What? What is this strange version of a story too familiar in his thoughts? What is this unexpected combination of these names? Stop! He will re-read the letter with forced patience, lest he be mistaken. Not one previous word of loss, embarrassment, or risk in any of the Locksley's own affairs? No, not an intimation. But it seems that Keane—yes, there it is, in black and white, in Lucy Locksley's hand—Keane was in league or partnership with Walter Sherbrooke, junior, had thrown the game up, had absconded, had been heard of from New York.

Let him recall what passed between them both at Malta.

Down he sits, his head between his hands, as he was wont to puzzle out some case made intricate by perjuries, and reserved from his cutcherry court, in Trans-Nerbuddah times.

The understanding of a noble heart is sensitive to light of good. One second's flash will print on it the meaning of a noble deed. But glare of evil finds the surface dull. It must have time to photograph on such the outline of a baser act.

At last, he saw the truth.

Thank God! His father's mind had not belied its nobleness!

How could the instinct of his own have thus belied its perfect trust in him?

Meanwhile, his hand, with nimblest, gentlest eagerness, had pushed its way beneath whatever folds lay on his breast, and it had grasped the locket hanging there. Delicious hope!

By dawn, on the twenty-ninth of December, the British army crossed the Kohuree. Valliant's brigade, with Littler in support, was launched on Chonda, defended by a triple intrenchment and a powerful artillery. By one of those strange oversights, or strange deceptions, which occur in war, the village of Maharajpore itself was not known to be filled, or ready for filling, by formidable masses of the enemy. But a cannonade, of which the first trial shots exposed to imminent danger the British general's own wife and other ladies with the civilians of the expedition, soon burst out of the clumps of trees and houses to undeceive the columns in the rear. Littler must turn his movement in support into a daring onslaught, beginning thus the day. The fight was stern and bloody. But Valliant's troops, changing their front at Sir Hugh Gough's command, bore down in reverse on the contested village. Their bayonets and Littler's silenced the guns, whose unexpected fire had wrought confusion in the British plan of battle; twenty-eight fell there into the power of this undaunted infantry. Meanwhile, upon the left, Scott, with unequal forces, contained, then broke, then swept away the horse of the Mahrattas. There rode Ned Locksley, there the one-eyed Jemadar, there, with an equal spirit though with unequal seat, brave Sergeant-Major Wilmot, and with him, on a spare charger of their leader's, the bold tiger tracking Bheel. Spite of their ancient cavalry renown, the Gwalior horsemen are tumbled back upon the batteries which flank the right of their own army, whose desperate gunners still serve their guns with unquailing hearts. Locksley's Horse are at an easy canter; but the cool practised eye of Ned has measured the just interval at which to make a rush and clear the sand-bags right into the batteries.

"Gallop!"

The Kattiwaree rises on his hind legs wildly,

paws the air, and falls back, his rider under him.

The battery is carried. So that they have not far to bear him out of reach of the dropping matchlock fire, which the brave Mahrattas will not even yet entirely give over. There was a tope of trees, and a fragment of a mud wall; both bore the crashing marks of cannon.

"Lay me down here, Tommy."

"I knowed he were hard hit, sir," would the Earl's head-keeper say, in aftertimes at home, to Robert Locksley. "He were a very partickler officer, sir, for all he were so kind-hearted, were Master Ned, sir. He always said 'sergeant-major,' sir, just soldier-like. And so I knowed he were hard hit, sir, when he says to me, 'Tommy,' he says, like as was of old times, here at Cransdale, sir."

They leaned him up against the little broken wall. Then the Bheel, at Nusreddeen's word, ran to fetch a little water and some bearers from a neighbouring group of huts. With an effort Ned drew from his breast-flap his little Greek New Testament; but his hand faltered, and his eyes swam. He let it fall beside him. His breathing was heavy and interrupted. Wilmot and the one-eyed Jemadar held him, looking at each other in blank despair.

"Tommy! Tommy Wilmot!"

It was little louder than a whisper.

"Yes, dear Master Ned, sir," said the sergeant-major, bending his ear almost to touch his lips, whilst big salt tears went rolling down his long flaxen moustachioes.

"Give my love to—my father—mother, Tommy. Tell—I charge—forgive—my cousin Keane."

Then he was silent, till Wilmot heard him say—

"Lord! now lettest thou thy servant"—

But the froth and blood came bubbling up to choke the words upon his dying breath.

They buried him at sun-down.

"Put this in with him," said the old one-eyed Mussulman. It was the little Testament he had picked up. "Allah Kerim! God is merciful. He was a servant of the Book!"

"And put in this!"

"No, not that," said the sergeant-major.

It was his grandfather's sword.

"Allah Kebir!" the stern old trooper answered gravely, snapping the sword in two against his knee; "God is great! No bungler shall wield the weapon. He was a master of it."

Therewith he threw the pieces in beside Ned Locksley.

But Thakali, the Bheel's wife, sat on the ground the night long, by the grave, mourning and casting dust upon her head. Poor half-savage heart, yet wholly grateful! Lucy Locksley's would have clung to it. For ever, in the after years, it clung to any who kept or brought, in kindliness, remembrance of her soldier son.

For that, when Philip brought home as his countess her that had been Rosa Barrington, not his own mother's arms embraced her with more loving fervour. For that, did Lucy knit, through her, close correspondence with her cousin Florence, his early and discerning friend on Indian ground. For that, when Gervinus also brought a bride to visit Rookenham, Amy, for it was she, felt in her heart's core Lucy's tenderness.

The Roystons had a second son, to whom they craved her leave to give the name of Edward Locksley.

Her fingers, tremulous with advancing age, were busy with his brown curls, so like her own Ned's, as once again she talked with Lady Royston of him who lay beneath the mangoe trees.

"No, Constance dear, not even such a loss need

leave a mother's heart robbed of all consolation. Look on this forehead, where, with your kisses, you shower hopeful prayers. What if an angel touched your eyes to read on its white parchment this answer to him:—'He shall be tender-hearted, yet strong-souled, just in rule, brave in war, serving God, in faith of Christ.' What if beads of death-dew blurred all else, would not enough be written? Would you not say—'Thank God! His holy will be done?'"

THE END

CPSIA information can be obtained
at www.ICGtesting.com
Printed in the USA
LVHW040433110522
718423LV00002B/352

9 783375 001346